THE
SECOND
AMERICAN REVOLUTION/CIVIL
WAR

RICK JOYNER

MorningStar Publications
www.MorningStarMinistries.org

The Second American Revolution/Civil War
By Rick Joyner

©2021 2nd Printing

MorningStar Ministries, Fort Mill, SC. All rights reserved.

Distributed by MorningStar Publications, Inc.,
a division of MorningStar Fellowship Church
375 Star Light Drive, Fort Mill, SC 29715

www.MorningStarMinistries.org
1-800-542-0278

Cover and layout design: Carlie McKinley

ISBN: 978-1-60708-678-9
For a free catalog of MorningStar Resources, please call 1-800-542-0278

TABLE OF CONTENTS

Chapter 1
We Are At War

On December 14, 2018, I had a dream about a coming Second American Revolution/Civil War. In this dream I was shown a brief overview of American history from heaven's perspective. I was shocked at how differently heaven saw our history from any history I had ever read. However, heaven's perspective was so clear and understandable that I knew it was true, and we need to see this to understand what is happening in our time.

The dream began with various attacks coming upon our country now, and how God had prepared champions to counter each one. In the dream the champions were lined up at a golf course waiting to tee off. As it became their turn, an angel would approach them and tell them the evil they would find in the trees on the fairway they had been designated to play. I knew that the trees represented the deep roots in our country that these evil strongholds now had.

These champions that were being sent forth to attack these evil strongholds would know what they were to go after by what "teed them off." For example, if abortion or human trafficking specifically provoked them the most, then that was the evil they were to seek out to destroy.

In the dream, I was waiting in line to be sent to fight one of these enemies when I was approached by an angel and told that

I had a different assignment. I was then taken to a large device that was showing "A History of The American Republic from Heaven's Perspective."

As I watched this, I saw that if I walked across the face of this device to my right the times progressed toward the present. I decided to go to the end to see heaven's perspective on what was happening now. When I came to the present, there was a sentence written in brilliant golden letters: *"The Second American Revolution/Civil War is inevitable, it is right, and it will be successful."*

From what I had viewed, as I walked to see the present, I understood why this Revolution/Civil War was "inevitable" and why it was "right." As I stood pondering this, feeling that this might be the most important revelation I had ever been entrusted with, I woke up.

We are in the first stages of "The Second American Revolution/Civil War." I know this leads to many questions, such as: What are the sides? What are the issues? What is right about it? Most important of all, what does success in this war look like from heaven's perspective?

As the saying goes, "If we do not change our direction we will end up where we are headed." We don't have to be a prophet to see that we're headed for civil war, if not already into the first stages. Before the dream I felt that we still had a long way to go before it became "inevitable." In the dream, I saw that we had already crossed that line and it is now upon us. This meant that we need to change our strategy from trying to avoid it to winning it. To do this, we must have heaven's definition of what winning looks like.

To my surprise, from heaven's perspective, we did not win the Revolutionary War. From heaven's perspective, that war was about more than just gaining our independence from Great Britain—it was about liberty and a revolution in the government of men that would establish and maintain liberty and justice for all. Some significant things were accomplished in this war, but there were also some very basic ways that it fell far short of what heaven viewed as successful.

One major failure of the Revolutionary War was that if the Founders had truly believed that all men were created equal— what they declared to be the reason for seeking independence— then slavery would not have been possible. Their omission of this basic purpose for the creation of the American Republic made the Civil War inevitable.

If the Civil War had been successful according to heaven's perspective, then there would not have been a need for such things as the Civil Rights Movement or many of the conflicts we are still fighting. The Union may have prevailed in crushing the Southern rebellion and ending slavery, but it did not prevail in a way that established justice and equality for all. We will not accomplish our purpose as a nation until there is justice and liberty for all. This is why both the Revolutionary War and Civil War must be fought again until there is a "successful" conclusion that aligns us with our most basic purpose as a nation.

In the American Republic, liberty and justice are not just skewed because of race, they are also perverted by wealth, fame, politics, and other factors. If liberty and justice are distorted at all it will be in both directions. The wealthy may be able to afford lawyers that can get them out of just about anything, but their wealth can also make them targets. The same is true of the famous, the politically strong, etc. There are consequences to perverting justice that are very costly and will be paid by those who pervert justice.

Heaven does not expect anything on earth to be perfect in this age. In fact, The Scriptures state that even the best on the earth is but a shadow of the heavenly. However, when we are in the shadow of something we are very close to the real. The American Republic is called to be much closer to liberty and justice for all than we have yet attained. We are called to be an example of these to the nations, not an example of the dysfunction of government and justice that we have now become.

We must also have heaven's perspective on war. We tend to think of war as pitched battles between standing armies, but what is unfolding will not be like the Revolutionary War or the Civil War in that way. There are some parallels with those wars that will relate to our times, but many will not. However, this does not mean that what we are now facing will be easier. The whole world is entering the most trying times there has ever been. What we will be given to face them is a sure hope from above that the outcome will be "successful."

For the first part of this I will be elaborating on the things I was shown in this dream. Then we will apply them with more depth to present conditions and conflicts.

The media landscape of the present day is a map in search of a territory. – *J.G. Ballard*

Chapter 2
Seeing from Above

Heaven's perspective of war can be very different than our human perspective. We tend to see the battles, which side prevails, and then which side exerts its will over the other. Heaven tends to look at them as how justice or injustice prevails. War is an ultimate evil, but war is inevitable until the end of this age, just as we see them right to the end of the Book of Revelation.

There are times when an even worse evil would prevail without war, and so there are righteous wars. In these it would be unrighteous, and even evil, not to fight for what is right. However, in most wars there is a mixture of good and evil intent, prosecution of the war, and outcomes. In this age, there will be a mixture of good and evil in virtually everything. Because of this, if we wait to have perfect motives or perfect conditions, we will likely not do anything. The best solution to an issue can be just a little better than the worst solution. It takes wisdom to know what to do, but it often takes even more to know when to do it.

I understand that without having the experience that I had in the dream, you may find it difficult to have the level of conviction that I might have about some of these things. Some you may agree with inherently, and some you may disagree with. However, because of the nature of this dream,

I must be bolder than I've ever been about some things I am going to share.

The first part of this dream I was given was for understanding the strategy that will be successful in this war. There will be champions raised up that will go out to attack the specific evil strongholds in our nation. These evils were things like bigotry, greed, selfish ambition, hatred, rebellion, pride, etc. In the dream, all of these evils were in trees, which speaks of them having roots and branches. To defeat them, one must not waste time flailing at the branches, but rather put an ax to the root of the tree.

America is not the kingdom of God or the New Jerusalem. I have searched our history for evidence that we had a special covenant with God, and I have not found it. Men have made covenants with God for the nation, but that is not the biblical criteria for a covenant God is obligated to keep, even if made by a leader of a nation. Every covenant of God originated with God, not man, and there is a clear and supernatural demonstration that He made the covenant. I may have missed it, but I could not find this in our national history. That does not mean that America does not have a specific purpose from God.

There is much evidence that America was dedicated to God. Dedications can originate with man, and according to Scripture everything dedicated to God is holy, or sanctified. There are special benefits and judgments that come with such a dedication. The favor of God is worth more than any earthly treasure or other resource. However, because everything dedicated to God is holy, a nation dedicated to God cannot do some things other nations may be able to get away with.

Purpose is the greatest favor of God that we have received for this dedication. We were given a purpose to be a nation that demonstrated the liberty and justice that all people were created to have. It is written that **"where the Spirit of the Lord is, there is liberty" (see II Corinthians 3:17)**. This is why The Tree of the Knowledge of Good and Evil was put in the Garden. There could be no true obedience unless there was the freedom to disobey. Freedom and free will is at the core of what we were created to be.

Our founding documents are not Scripture, but they were inspired by God in order to reveal and lead us to our destiny. It is because we have this calling that when we drift from that many of the troubles we are not embroiled in have come. Having a clear vision of our destiny and getting back on the path to fulfilling it is crucial to our well-being, and even our continued existence as a Republic.

Our discord increases the more we deviate from our purpose. As discussed, one of our basic purposes as a nation was to establish a place where it is understood that "all men are created equal" and also *practiced*. In heaven, this, not independence, was the main issue with the Revolutionary War. Because our main purpose was compromised and hypocritically disregarded after the Revolutionary War, the Civil War became inevitable. If the American Republic had really believed that all men were created equal, then slavery, and even discrimination based on race, could not have remained possible here.

The Civil War may have ended slavery, at least in its most diabolical form, but it did not go as far as establishing that "all men are created equal." This is just one factor in our mandate that has yet to be fulfilled. We can be thankful for the progress that has been made in reducing discrimination in America, and there has been notable progress, but it is still far from the place we are called to be. We have now come to the point where increasing conflict is inevitable until we recover a clear vision of the mandate we were given as a nation and resolve to fully obey it.

What does that look like?

Don't believe everything you think. *—Byron Katie*

Chapter 3
A Battle for the Ages

What I was shown in my dream was specifically for "The American Republic," but I was also shown that many of the same battles we will be fighting will also be common to many nations. Basically, these battles in the nations are for determining whether they will be a "sheep" or a "goat" nation when The Lord returns to set up His kingdom. The Great Commission was to disciple nations, not just individuals, not only teaching them to believe all that He commanded, but also to obey all that He commanded.

The Reformation was a major step forward in recovering biblical truth, but its emphasis was more on believing the right things than actually doing them. All nations have fallen short of their purpose, including Israel as The Scriptures make clear. One reason the nations have fallen short is because there is so little demonstration of what actual obedience to the truth looks like by the church. This is why **"judgment begins with the household of God" (see I Peter 4:17)**.

As heaven's perspective on history and current events can be very different from ours, our basic devotion must be to see with The Lord's eyes, hear with His ears, and understand with His heart. This was what The Holy Spirit was given for, and this is how we are led into "all truth."

Most of us have witnessed spiritual battles that resulted in everything from church splits to divorces, and God was on both sides. God hates divorce, and He hates war. He almost always has sons and daughters on both sides, and in ways He can be on both sides. He's not confused about the issues, but He is for people more than politics.

God is not a Democrat or a Republican, a liberal or a conservative. We can be right in our political beliefs, but be wrong in spirit. We can likewise be wrong in our politics but have a right spirit of love, faith, and humility that pleases The Lord more than those who have right politics. This is why, to the confusion of many historians, there can be evidence of Divine favor on both sides during a war.

Abraham Lincoln discerned that our Civil War was God's judgment on both the North and the South. This might explain why the Union was obviously on the right side of some of the crucial issues being fought over, but the Southern armies experienced some of the greatest revivals in American history *during the war.*

How could it be that those who were fighting for such a terrible cause would be moved upon by God this way? Perhaps it is because the victors always get to write the history of wars, and some of the real issues of this conflict have been overlooked or changed by historians to make their cause seem more noble. I think as we dig down into understanding both our Revolutionary and Civil Wars we will find this to be at least part of the distortion.

Perhaps The Lord moved so mightily upon the Southern armies because **"where sin abounds grace does that much more abound" (see Romans 5:20)**, and He was seeking to change their hearts on the issues. Perhaps it was because it is often true that those who can be right on issues are wrong in spirit, and God will always resist the proud and give His grace to the humble. It was likely a combination of both of these and other issues that we can benefit from understanding.

The point is that we like to have all issues neatly in black and white, but human issues are almost always far more complicated than that. We are in desperate need of heaven's perspective. The higher the place that we can see from, the more sense it will all make.

In the Revolutionary and Civil Wars, both sides were fighting for parts of the Divine mandate on the nation. It was the arrogance of the victors in both of these wars that blinded them to just and righteous issues for which the other side was fighting. Neither side was totally right or wrong, but the victors disregarded the consideration that the losers might have been right about some of the issues. Such is human politics. Since the victors always write the histories of such conflicts, the just issues on the losing side are often buried after a war. We can bury them as deep as we want, but when they are a Divine mandate they will not go away. Rather, they will rise again and be in our face until they are resolved by our obeying them.

It is also easy to see how these same principles might apply to all human relationships. We can win an argument because we are mostly right, but be wrong about some of it. Those issues we were wrong about will very likely surface again later, and often as a bigger problem. The revelation of the great conflict of our times includes principles that may illuminate the basis for our conflict in other more personal relationships, such as our families, jobs, or neighborhoods. We cannot expect to resolve the great national and international conflicts if we cannot solve them in ourselves, our families, or in the church.

When I spoke to a number of senators and congressmen in Washington a few years ago, I entreated them to show courage in standing boldly for their convictions. After my speech, a couple of these took me aside and said, "You would see a lot more courage in Washington if we saw any in the church." They were right.

It's been said that "Courage is the first principle of leadership, because without it nothing else will stand." We have come to a time when courage is rare, and that makes it even more valuable. Perhaps this is why the cowards are the first to get thrown into the lake of fire at the end of the Book of Revelation. We may think that love and faith are more important, and they are, but courage is the evidence that one has true love and true faith, not just doctrines about them.

As we are told in I Corinthians 13:8, **"Love never fails."** This could have been interpreted as "Love never quits." We will quit for any other reason but love. This is why the foundation of those who will be on the winning side will be love for their country and for their countrymen. However, most of all it will be love for God who has given us such great grace and favor as a nation, even if we yet have flaws.

It is never too late to be what you might have been. – *George Eliot*

Chapter 4
A Time for War

Wars have been fought for many different reasons. There have been religious, political, and economic wars. Some have been just for conquest. Some have been fought because one monarch was insulted by another, which is why Napoleon invaded Russia. Many have been fought over combinations of these, or even other issues. Some of the ugliest and devastating of all have been racist wars.

Every war is the result of some failure in human relations. Devastating wars have also been avoided by remarkable statesmanship. The Lord has a special heart and place for the peacemakers. These should be esteemed more in our history than those successful at war, but they are not. Even so, as we are told in Ecclesiastes 3, there is a time for war and a time for peace. If it is time for war, then those who do not fight are the ones out of step with the times. We cannot walk in truth in some basic ways if we are out of step with the times.

As we see in Scripture, there will be war until the end of this age. Even so, it is right to seek peaceful conclusions to our disputes, until war begins. Then we must fight, and we must fight to win. If we are going to win from heaven's perspective, we must also fight for the right reasons, and we must fight the right way.

Some of the most touching stories of war are things like the troops on both sides in our American Civil War, and in

World War I, singing Christmas carols to their enemies during the Christmas season. It brought a poignant realization that brothers in Christ were facing each other, and the next day would try to kill each other. How could this be right?

War is an ultimate evil and an ultimate human failure. War is one of the devil's biggest victories. His intent is to kill and destroy, and nothing accomplishes this in a bigger way than war. So why don't we refuse to fight them? Because the devil, and those controlled by him, will continue to fight and will prevail if the good do not continue to fight. To refuse to fight in an inevitable or right war is not choosing to do what is right. Rather, it is to submit to evil. There are righteous wars. When it is right and time to fight, we will be in rebellion if we do not do our part.

Even The Lord says repeatedly in Scripture that He, our Leader, is a Warrior. Israel left Egypt as "a great mixed multitude," or a mob, but before they even got to the Red Sea they were "marching in martial array." That means they were marching in military order. Presently, the body of Christ is far more like a mob than a disciplined military force. We may have some groupings and associations but are lacking in overall definition and discipline. This must change.

In every civil war, Christian leaders from both sides have claimed that theirs was the right side. This can obviously be confusing. We must resolve to be sure we are fighting on the right side and for the right cause. When this is established, the most merciful way is to fight to win decisively and as quickly as possible.

Harry Truman was right when he said that "Most people are defeated by their secondary successes." This means that they got distracted from their ultimate objective after achieving lesser ones. There are many examples of this in history, and Truman was likely correct to say this happens to "most people." It was true in our Revolutionary and Civil Wars. How do we avoid this deadly trap? We must determine now what the ultimate objectives are and resolve that anything less than accomplishing these is not acceptable.

I have an opinion of what ultimate victory in the unfolding Revolution/Civil War looks like, but I don't want to share it and I don't even want to have it. What we need, and what I'm begging for, is heaven's perspective on this. My dream on December 14, 2018 was just a small beginning of this for me. It does not matter how mature we are in Christ or how successful we have been as a steward of His mysteries—it is a terrible presumption to think that He is just like us and that His opinions are the same as ours. I am a religious conservative, and I try to keep in mind that it was the religious conservatives that were the worst enemies of Christ when He walked the earth. Why?

If you look at their doctrine, the Pharisees were generally correct in most of their beliefs. They were the most devoted to being faithful to The Scriptures and were carrying the greatest hope for the Messiah. Yet, they resisted Him more than any other group when He came! Why?

Again, we can be right in our politics, our policies, and our beliefs, but have a pride that is deadlier than the evil we are fighting. Pride caused the first fall and virtually every fall since. We can be right but not be righteous. For winning the present war, it is crucial to not just fight for what is right, but to do it in the right spirit. We must fight for right and we must do it right.

In the Revolutionary War, the "Patriots" who wanted independence were about 30% of the population. The "Loyalists" who wanted to remain British subjects were also about 30%. The other 40% were undecided, or tended to switch sides according to who was winning. Today, we have about 30% who are liberal, 30% conservative, and the 40% that are still undecided or wavering. Soon all will have to choose a side. Now is the time to resolve what we believe in, and what we believe in enough to fight for. In what is unfolding everyone will be on one side or the other, as the middle ground will not continue to exist.

The problem is not to find the answer; it's to face the answer. *—Terence McKenna*

Chapter 5
The Strategy

In the dream that I was given about the "Second American Revolution/Civil War," the first part was about the strategy for this war. The symbolism may seem odd, but if you stick with me for a little bit, it gives important insights into what we must do now.

As I shared previously, the dream began with a long line of people waiting to tee off at a golf course. After each one teed off, they were told about the enemy they were to look for to destroy. This enemy was in the trees along the fairway. I was waiting in line for my turn when an angel came up to me and said I had a different assignment. That's when I was taken to the device that revealed the history of the American Republic from heaven's perspective.

Golf, like many sports and games, can be a mirror of life. The goal is to get the ball in a hole that has a flag, or standard, over it. Each hole on the course is different from the others. In golf no two shots will be the same, as you will always be at least a slightly different distance from your target, or have different weather conditions, or even different conditions of the course itself. So, you must judge several conditions on each shot, such as distance to the hole, wind, and elevation. You may know exactly what you should do, but actually doing it the way you want is another matter. To be successful, you need to stay in the fairway, or let's say "the way." If you go too far to either the right or left, you will go out of bounds and that brings a serious penalty.

I don't want to bore you with a golf lesson here, but having played golf for many years, this part of the dream made perfect sense to me as a strategy for winning the Revolution/Civil War. To some degree, if we are going to understand prophetic symbolism, we must learn that The Lord likes to use puns. We are told in Psalm 2:4 that **"He who sits in the heavens laughs."** This may be because He thinks they are funny, but they can also powerfully convey an understanding about His perspective on things.

In this dream, those who were teeing off were going to find the enemy they were assigned to destroy. This insight about what "tees us off," or deeply agitates us, will be what we are called to fight. These are not random provocations intended to irritate us; they are calls to action. We must all consider how we can be a part of fighting what provokes us the most and what Scripture defines as evil.

Again, for Christians The Scriptures are clear that our battle is never against people, but rather against the demonic forces that are manifested through ideologies and deceptions that bind, and ultimately, destroy them. Our victory is not to kill and wound, but to heal and lead people to the path of life. We are not fighting to conquer people or to just win the argument, but we fight to establish the truth that sets people free.

How does that work when a spiritual or philosophical war breaks out into violence? These are the kinds of issues we need to settle in our hearts now because the confused are almost certain to be casualties in what is unfolding.

We may also think that if God hates war then His people should stay out of every conflict. God does hate war, but as we briefly discussed before, He is declared to be a warrior in a number of Scriptures. No doubt that if we followed Him more fully, our disputes would not come to war. However, as we are told in Ecclesiastes 3, there is a time for war. There are times when war is inevitable, and times when it is right to fight. What I was shown in the dream is that this Second American Revolution/ Civil War is *inevitable*, it is *right*, and it will be *successful*.

At this writing I still do not know what or how it happened, but in this dream we had just crossed a line that made this Second Revolution/Civil War inevitable. There will not be a peaceful solution to the conflicts that have arisen in our country. Even so, I will continually pray that this be won decisively and with the fewest possible casualties and the least damage as possible.

Why this is called a Revolution and Civil War is important. Much of what we need to understand the great battles of our times lies in understanding these conflicts. This is because so much of what was fought over before was not decisively concluded in the conflicts because they were compromised in order to gain a faster peace.

War is so terrible this is understandable, but it is not acceptable. After the spectacular victory of Israel over Jericho as they began to fight for their Promised Land, they were then defeated before the tiny little village of Ai. This happened because there was compromise and sin within the camp of Israel. Until this was dealt with they were vulnerable before their enemies. When they found the culprit, and justice was meted out, Joshua learned that as long as he held out his javelin, Israel would prevail against their enemies. If he withdrew the javelin, their enemies prevailed. So, Joshua held out the javelin until their enemies were completely destroyed, not just pushed back. We must do the same with the evil strongholds that are now occupying our land.

Wars come in many forms. The Cold War brought about perhaps the greatest geopolitical change in history; however, it was not fought with traditional weapons, but rather with banks and currencies. It was an economic war more than a political or military one. Just as in the Revolutionary and Civil Wars, many of the issues that the Cold War was fought over were not decisively defeated, and now they have risen to face us again.

We must not forget that the most powerful weapons of all are the "divinely powerful weapons" that we have been entrusted with. Truth articulated under the anointing is more powerful than any bomb. Though there will be physical conflict in what is now unfolding, the most important issues will be the spiritual and moral ones, especially our devotion to liberty for all—that everyone be treated equally and fairly under the law and with opportunity.

Don't fear failure. Not failure, but low aim is the crime. In great attempts it is glorious even to fail. –*Bruce Lee*

Chapter 6
Awakening and War

Even a cursory study of history reveals that many of the issues over which the American Revolutionary and Civil Wars were fought are still far from being settled, and continue to be points of conflict in our country. Many of the issues have evolved and are not in the exact same form, but basically, our present struggle continues to be about independence, liberty, freedom from the bondage of oppressive government, or any other oppressor, and equal justice under the law—for all.

How does this fit with the next Great Awakening that so many have prophesied, including myself? The First Great Awakening preceded the Revolutionary War. The Second Great Awakening preceded the Civil War. It is easy to see a direct link between the messages of these Great Awakenings and how they ignited these wars.

The light of these Awakenings exposed darkness to the degree that it could no longer be tolerated. Likewise, the light already being revealed from the emerging Awakening in this time is causing great agitation in our land. The issues have morphed in a lot of ways, but they are basically the same ones that were fought over in the Revolutionary and Civil Wars.

Some historians concluded that the American Revolution began when George Whitefield was forbidden to preach in the Church of England and began preaching in open fields to the common people in the 1730s. This was almost half a century before the Revolutionary War, but sometimes seeds take a while to germinate, sprout, and bear fruit. So how did the light that Whitefield brought sow the seeds of American independence?

Whitefield began preaching to the common people in a town of coal miners. This village was considered so lowly they considered themselves too unworthy to even have a church in their town. To the shock of all who heard Whitefield, especially these miners, he began to declare that they were the true royalty in the earth—"the royal priesthood"—if they gave their lives to Christ and followed Him. In the class-sensitive England of the time, this was shocking and revolutionary.

These lowly miners could not fathom being allowed to get within sight of the royal family, yet Whitefield was telling them that if they were in Christ, they were of even higher royal stature than the British royal family. This seed became the doctrine that "all men are created equal," and that who we are in spirit, in relation to Christ, is more important than any earthly, human lineage.

As the Apostle Paul wrote, we should therefore no longer judge people after the flesh—after externals—but after the Spirit. As Martin Luther King, Jr. later paraphrased this, he had a dream that we would not judge each other by the color of our skin, but by the content of our character. That we would be a nation where this is true, the real "American dream" and one that heaven has given to us.

So, Whitefield's messages implied that the poorest miner who followed Christ was of a higher stature than any earthly royalty. These miners gave their lives to Him by the thousands. Soon Whitefield, who had filled many churches with the hundreds who sought to hear him, now had trouble finding fields big enough to hold the thousands who sought to hear this message.

It was not just Whitefield's remarkable ability as an orator that drew the crowds, but also a foundational aspect of the Gospel that for centuries had not been so articulated. Once again "the poor had the Gospel preached to them." There is nothing on earth as revolutionary as the Gospel of Jesus Christ. When it is preached, revolution is inevitable—even where it is claimed to already be Christian. There can be a big difference between institutional Christianity and the true faith.

When Whitefield brought to the colonies this message that so elevated "the common man," the crowds swelled to tens of thousands. Many of his crowds were larger than the population of the cities in which he preached. People would travel for days or even weeks to hear him. They drove their buggies, rode their mules and horses, and even walked to hear the great evangelist when it was published that he would be in a certain city on a certain date.

Whitefield also preached in humble, small churches. He did not seem to be a respecter of people or crowd size. Some of these small meetings may have had as much impact on the destiny of the nation as the larger ones. When he spoke at the Polegreen Church just north of Richmond, Virginia, the little church of less than a hundred people later became known as "the womb of the Revolution."

Sitting in that small audience were some destined to be called the fathers of the nation. Patrick Henry was one of those. He lived only a few hundred yards from the Polegreen Church, but the passion for liberty born in him that day would soon fire the nation.

Again, the main seed that sprouted and became a revolution was the Gospel that elevated the common man to being sons and daughters of The King of kings. This was the seed that became the message that "all men are created equal." This led to the previously unimagined concept that government existed for the people and not the other way around.

In the world at that time, there was no other place and no other government that considered this concept. This was the basis for what is called "American exceptionalism." To be exceptional does not necessarily mean better, but rather just different. In this case, it was better. The American Republic became the exception to every other government in the world, and soon a marvel to the world even in its formative, immature years.

This is why many historians believe that the First Great Awakening was the beginning of the Revolutionary War. However, the Revolutionary War did not win this freedom for all and did not result in all men being treated equally. A whole class of people were still treated worse than the coal miners that Whitefield had first preached this message to. This made an even more devastating war necessary, and the revolution continues to this day.

You miss 100% of the shots you don't take. –*Wayne Gretzky*

Chapter 7
The Main Thing

Peter Lord used to remind us often that "the main thing is to keep the main thing the main thing." This remains a fundamental truth that can keep us on course.

The "main thing," or the ultimate issue of both the Revolutionary and Civil Wars, can be summed up in one word—LIBERTY. True freedom requires liberty and justice for all, but there will be no justice where there is no liberty. We are still fighting for these, and this war will not be over until they are realized as fully as they can be on this earth. To pursue this is the calling and destiny of the American Republic, and every American.

The Divine wisdom given to our American Founding Fathers that became our Constitution and Bill of Rights was for a government structure that contained built-in relief valves—ones that enabled the peaceful settling of injustices and infringement on our freedoms. Departure from the wisdom in these founding documents is the reason for virtually every conflict and crisis we are now facing as a nation. These will not be resolved without reconnecting to The Constitution and Bill of Rights. For this reason, the ultimately successful strategy in the Second American Revolution/Civil War will be to fight for their restoration as "the supreme law of the land."

Both major American political parties, the left and the right, are guilty of failing to keep their vows to defend The Constitution. Neither party is now capable of recovering what has been lost in our "constitutional republic." A new movement is coming that will restore The Constitution to its rightful place so that we can become the nation we are called to be. The Second American Revolution/Civil War will be to complete what was begun by the first ones, and it will be led by a "third column" that is bigger than our present issues.

As stated previously, the First and Second Great Awakenings preceded the Revolutionary and Civil Wars respectively. The messages that came out of those Awakenings caused those wars, but before the conflicts erupted they presented an even higher way, which if followed, those wars could have been avoided.

If the political leaders of the time had truly embraced the truths of those Awakenings and had the courage to obey them, both of those wars could have been avoided and the trajectory of our nation toward our calling and destiny would have been much easier and cleaner. As we see from the beginning of history until now, men rarely choose the best way, but seek what they perceive to be the easiest way. However, this inevitably results in a far more costly conflict.

Great Britain, which lost the American colonies to a large degree because of the hardliners in Parliament, learned their lesson. While led by some of the same people whose hardline response to the grievances of the colonies caused the Revolutionary War, they softened to the message raised by William Wilberforce about the evils of slavery and eradicated it in the Empire without a great war.

That which can be accomplished without war is always preferable. However, when the political leadership is not capable of this, then war is preferable to allow evil not to prevail. We must come to grips with this now. Our federal government is dysfunctional and not capable of resolving the great conflicts now rising. Neither has there been the kind of transcendent leadership to emerge to restore the dysfunctional federal government and lead through such a crisis as is now upon us.

So, what do we do? We each do what we can in our sphere of influence. If we are one of the champions being called to confront the evil of our times, we must engage. If we are not one of the leaders then perhaps we are called to join those who are, but all of us are called to be engaged—the salt and light that has been given to the world.

We can expect the voices that arise calling for the New American Revolution to be blamed for the rising discord, just as Elijah was called the one who troubled Israel. Yet, sin and corruption are the true cause of the trouble, not what exposes them.

Unity is a wonderful thing, but not when it comes at the cost of tolerating or allowing evil to subjugate the people. There is a point when it is no longer possible to avoid conflict. When that line has been crossed, our strategy must change from keeping the peace to winning the war. That line has now been crossed in "The American Republic." It may take a while for others to see this, but it will soon be obvious.

When it is settled that the "Second American Revolution/ Civil War is *inevitable, right,* and will be *successful,*" the next step in our preparation is to determine what is "right" about it, and what "successful" looks like from heaven's perspective. For the truth to accomplish its purpose in these times it must transcend mere human wisdom—we must have wisdom from above. Thankfully, this is promised to those who will ask for it.

According to I Corinthians 13 we see in part, we know in part, and we prophesy in part. I only have part of the picture of what is unfolding. I am confident in this part, but not if it is not rightly joined with the parts others have been given. When I inquired of The Lord about His vision and His purpose for our nation, His response was that He gave it to our leaders in the beginning. It was articulated in our founding documents, and it is in them that we must see many of the parts we do not now have.

About two decades ago I began a study to see if I could find a special covenant or mandate that God had given to our country. My prayer for this was Psalm 90:16-17: **"Let Your work appear to Your servants and Your majesty to their children. Let the favor of the Lord our God be upon us; and confirm for us the work of our hands; yes, confirm the work of our hands."** I asked to see His hand and guidance in the founding of our nation, and by this understand His purpose so that our work and prayers for the country would be toward the fulfillment of His purpose.

In my study, I was surprised by how obvious His handiwork could be seen in our nation's founding. It was also easy to see the serious trouble we suffered as we deviated from His purpose. We are now entering the worst crises in our history when it will be determined if we will live or die as the Republic we have been called to be. If there is anything worth fighting for in our life, it is God's purpose. If there is anything worth fighting for in our nation, it is God's purpose for our nation.

Work begins when the fear of doing nothing at all finally trumps the terror of doing it badly. –*Alain de Botton*

Chapter 8

The Whole Message of This Life

Over the last 30+ years I've been given dreams that I now understand relate to the reason for the Second American Revolution/Civil War. I did not see them as such when I received them, but since my dream on December 14, 2018, they have all come into remarkable focus as pieces of a big picture. I will share these in this study where they fit to help us relate to what is now unfolding.

In 1987, I was shown in a prophetic experience that we had been turning to the left as a nation for a long time. I was also shown a coming sharp turn to the left. I was not shown whether this was good or bad, just that it would happen. I was then shown a reaction to this and a turn back to the right. I saw that we would never again make a sharp turn to the left, but there was a danger that we would go too far to the right.

I wrote about this in my book, *The Harvest*. That is also when I was told that an eagle needs both a right wing and a left wing to fly. When the weight shifted to the extreme on either wing it could not continue to fly. So, the warning was that extreme turns to the right or left could bring us down.

A few years after this, I thought that the extreme turn to the left was with the Clinton Administration. Then I was sure it had to be the Obama Administration that turned the country much further to the left than Clinton. The Trump Administration seems to be the beginning of turning back to the right. Now we have the rise of the new socialists that seem even further to the left than the Obama Administration. Could they be the ones who make the extreme turn to the left that I saw coming? Perhaps.

Regardless, the extreme turn to the left brought such a reaction in the country that there was a turn back to the right, and there would never again be a turn back to the left here. However, they can still do the nation much harm by causing a reaction to tempt us to go even further to the right than we should. The extremes on both the right and the left are enemies of what we are called to be.

So, will the right or the left lead us to our destiny, our Promised Land? Neither will. Something much higher than either of these is coming. With the increasingly extreme political clamor, it is going to take a new generation of transcendent leadership to both see and steer us toward our destiny and purpose. The vision that we need is much higher than presently found with either the right or the left. This is the "third column" that is going to emerge.

I've studied history for over half a century, and I've never seen in any country or at any single time such remarkable leaders gathered in one place at the same time as I saw in our Founding Fathers. With the possible exception of a mature Lincoln—who he was at the end of his life—it could be argued that we have not had such transcendent leaders since our founding as a nation. What we need now, and what we will be given again, is not just one transcendent leader, but another group of them so that together they will be considered the "new Founding Fathers."

We can also expect some of these to be mothers. The mother element is necessary to see the full vision of what we're called to be. The only commandment God gave that had a promise attached was to honor our fathers and mothers. We will have more to say about this later, but no one can be a father without a mother being present. We must also esteem and honor mothers and motherhood as one of the remarkable gifts God has given us, and that we cannot be who we are created to be without fathers and mothers being honored as they should.

Somehow, we must stop thinking right and left, and start thinking "up." We also need to see our place in The Scriptures, such as Revelation 12:13-16:

> **And when the dragon saw that he was thrown down to the earth, he persecuted the woman who gave birth to the man child.**
>
> **But the two wings of the great eagle were given to the woman, so that she could fly into the wilderness to her place, where she was nourished for a time and times and half a time, from the presence of the serpent.**
>
> **And the serpent poured water like a river out of his mouth after the woman, so that he might cause her to be swept away with the flood.**
>
> **But the earth helped the woman, and the earth opened its mouth and drank up the river which the dragon poured out of his mouth.**

Until the Advent Movement of 1844, this text was almost universally believed by Protestants and evangelical movements to be speaking about America. The woman here is considered to be who the Apostle Paul referred to as "Jerusalem above who is our mother." The male child who will rule the nations is Christ, who was born through the nation of Israel and is now being born through the church of those who have been born of Christ by the Spirit.

During the Inquisition, the worst persecution against Protestants and Jews in which it was estimated that as many as 50 million in Europe were tortured and killed, the "earth opened" with the discovery of America. This flood of persecution was then swallowed up as the nations of Europe gave their attention to populating this "new world."

Of course, the symbol of the United States is the eagle. In the text, we see that "two wings of a great eagle" were given to help the woman, the church, who was carried to a wilderness, which is what America was at that time. Many, if not most, of the first colonists were Protestant Christians and Jews fleeing the persecution of the Inquisition in Europe.

For this reason, it seems that one of our basic purposes as a nation is to be a haven for the persecuted Christians and Jews. To this day, Christians and Jews remain the most persecuted people in the world. This is not to say that we should not be a haven for other persecuted peoples, but a main purpose that we have is to be a haven for persecuted Christians and Jews, the people who have carried the seed of Christ—the "man-child."

For this reason, the American Republic is called to be a Judeo-Christian nation. We are not a post-Christian nation, we are a pre-Christian nation. Wait and see.

Try again. Fail again. Fail better. −*Samuel Beckett*

Chapter 9
Timing

One of the questions I am asked the most about this coming Second American Revolution/Civil War is when it will break out. I have not personally received anything about the timing of this. However, several prophetic people have given words that civil war would break out in America in 2021. A rationale some have given for this is that Trump will be elected to a second term and this will exacerbate our divisions into violence. Perhaps. It seems that the divisions are so great in the country that if either side wins the 2020 election it will lead to conflict.

I regularly hear words that are attributed to me that I never gave. They are often the opposite of what I believe. This has been the case with prophecy from the beginning, and we see it with many of the biblical prophets—they had to contend with words from others that countered theirs. This is why it is increasingly important for us to not just seek to hear words from The Lord, but to hear The Word Himself. We must know His voice and follow The Lamb, not just prophetic words. The Lord is our Shepherd, not any man, and not any prophet.

Something like a Revolution/Civil War is so dramatic, and its consequences so great, that it can overshadow almost everything else. However, the most important event now unfolding in our country is another Great Awakening. With the Awakening, we can expect revivals to break out in different parts of the country as well as a great spiritual hunger to know The Lord. This is far more important than the Revolution/Civil War and will be a main factor in the outcome of this conflict.

Things in the natural often parallel what is happening in the Spirit, and there is also a great revolution beginning in the church. Like the revolution that will restore The Constitution as "the supreme law of the land," a great revolution is coming to the church to restore it to the solid biblical foundation of what church life is intended to be, and even what real Christianity is.

Presently, only a small fraction of U.S. citizens have read The Constitution and Bill of Rights, even among the many officials elected and appointed that are required to take an oath to defend it from all enemies foreign and domestic. Our ministry's lawyer took Constitutional Law in law school and his class never once referred to The Constitution. They spent all of their time studying Supreme Court decisions because the Supreme Court has usurped the place of The Constitution as the supreme law of the land. This has become the source of the biggest divisions growing in our country.

Likewise, the church is filled with teachers and teaching that is disconnected from The Scriptures, most of it being the teaching of human thinking and wisdom. One popular evangelical journal did a study of what it was publishing and found that less than one percent of the articles they published had even one reference to Scripture. This is from the church movement that prides itself the most on being devoted to The Scriptures. Spurgeon once said that he could find ten men who would die for The Bible for every one that would read it! It's still true.

There has never been anything, and never will be anything, as revolutionary as the Gospel of the kingdom of Jesus Christ. This is the Gospel that Jesus and His disciples preached, but it has not truly been preached since. There has never been anything written—and never will be—as revolutionary as The Bible. Just as we can point to the departure from our Constitution as the root of virtually every crisis in our government and country, we can likewise point to the root of the great crises in Christianity and the church to our deviation from sound, biblical truth. The main answer to the crises in our country and the church is to return to the foundations given to us in The Constitution and The Bible.

The most important thing we can do to be prepared for the times is to:

1. Get closer to The Lord, know Him as our Shepherd.

2. Get to know His voice better for our personal guidance, as He said in John 10 that His sheep know His voice.

3. Find our place in His body, the church. According to I Corinthians 10 and 11, the only reason Christians are weak, sick, or die prematurely is because they do not discern The Lord's body.

4. Get the teaching, training, and equipping that we need to function in our ministry, which every Christian has.

5. Get to know The Bible for ourselves.

Some of the most popular doctrines embraced by Christians today are not found in The Bible, and many are even contrary to its teachings. Peter warned about the teachings that, **"the untaught and unstable distort, just as they do also the rest of the Scriptures, to their own destruction" (II Peter 3:16)**. The foolishness of so many to follow those who are pretenders and disconnected from the truth is the cause of much of the destruction that we are headed for.

When a politician today challenges something as "unconstitutional," more often than not what they are promoting is in fact unconstitutional. Likewise, the same is true of church leaders declaring something to be biblical, or not, when the opposite of what they're saying is true.

When asked about the signs of the end of the age, the first thing The Lord said was "Don't be deceived." Many of the other prophecies about the end of this age highlight how deception will be a primary mark of this time. It seems from any perspective we must conclude that we are there now.

The antidote? Obey the Great Commission and make disciples, not just converts. We must have the wisdom and the nobility of the Bereans who searched The Scriptures for themselves to check out what the apostles were teaching. Those who continue to trust others to know The Lord and His voice for them are going to become increasingly open to deception.

We must resolve to study what Jesus said about His disciples. A true disciple of Christ has knowing their Master, learning of Him, and becoming like Him, doing the works that He did, as the greatest focus of their life. This type of radical, revolutionary Christianity is about to be released on the earth again. The most important thing we can do to prepare for what is coming is to become His disciple, according to His definition of what that is.

I attribute my success to this: I never gave or took any excuse. –*Florence Nightingale*

Chapter 10
The Ultimate Revolution

For fifty years I have had dreams, visions, and revelations about the coming revolutions and civil wars in the church. I have written extensively about these, and my most popular books have been about them. What I understood, but did not give too much attention to, is how closely events in the natural parallel what is happening in the Spirit. Connecting these better will help us prepare for both, and prevail in both.

When we begin to glimpse the kingdom of God and the city that God is building, it is hard to consider anything happening on the earth as important. I really get this, but nevertheless, what is happening now must be important to us now if we are going to be a part of preparing for His coming kingdom.

The emerging spiritual awakening is also imperative for the Revolution/Civil War to be successful in the natural. As our national Founding Fathers declared, the Republic they gave to us only works for a moral and religious people, and they admitted that it was "inadequate for governing any others." There is no way to have a successful outcome in our country's coming Revolution/Civil War if the revolution in the church does not precede it.

We can reconnect our government to The Constitution that embodies God's wisdom for government, but without a spiritual Awakening in America, it will not be long before it is disconnected again and lawlessness prevails. Our Constitution is not a law that forces righteousness, but it is the construction of a limited government that protects its people from evil and promotes liberty.

The Founders were right: our Constitutional Republic can only work for those who want to do what is right because of a strong religious and moral compass in their heart. Therefore, they are given the ability to choose what is right because they love God, righteousness, and justice, and also love, honor, and respect one another.

This may sound too good to work for any civil government, and it is without devotion to God and high moral principles by the people governed. In this age of increasing lawlessness, immorality, greed, and all other forms of perversion and darkness, this may seem even more unrealistic. It is more than unrealistic— it is impossible with men. However, we must never forget that:

"Nothing is impossible for God."

The Lord is not challenged by what may seem impossible for us. The biblical record and history reveal that He does His best work when the challenge is the most impossible for us. The Christian life He has called us to is not just the most difficult life we can live—it is impossible. No human being can live the Christian life we are called to without Christ! He designed what He called us to as impossible without Him.

No human life on this planet can be successful without God. He made man to need Him. We can accomplish what is in our heart without Him, but if such get the chance to ponder their life on their deathbed, they will know it was frivolous, empty, and a failure at what was truly important. Has there yet been anyone on their deathbed who had remorse that they did not make more money, build or accumulate more stuff, or get more of the attention or accolades of men?

God is asking us to do the impossible. He wants the American Republic to be a government that will not work without Him. Like Israel of old that had to learn over and over that they could not survive without God, we are now there ourselves. We will not last much longer without Him. We simply cannot survive as a secular nation. The further we have moved in that direction, the further we have tottered over the precipice of our demise.

As we see in Revelation 11:15, when the seventh trumpet sounds, which is the seventh and last message that goes forth, the kingdoms of this world will become the kingdom of our Lord. There is a transition being prepared, a bridge to the age to come. This is why we are told in Isaiah 40 that we prepare the way for The Lord by building a highway. This highway is God's "higher-way."

The Lord has a higher way, higher than even man's greatest wisdom, to do just about everything. This includes government, education, business—everything. To the degree that we align ourselves with His ways is the degree to which we build what can last, upon His kingdom that cannot be shaken.

The Founders of the American Republic developed a Constitution for a republic that would limit government, not promote the expansion of it. They understood that anything the government did for its citizens beyond three basic areas would come with strings attached that would ultimately have the people in bondage again.

The three areas they believed civil government needed to have authority over was for the common defense, foreign affairs, and interstate commerce. All other authority in The

Constitution was remanded "to the states and to the people." When our federal government went beyond its constitutional mandate, virtually every crisis we're now facing began to grow.

As C.S. Lewis wrote, "When you make a wrong turn and get on the wrong road it will never turn into the right road. The only way to get on the right road is to go back to where you missed the turn." We may think that it is impossible to go back to those now. It is if we're looking to the right or the left, but not if we're looking up. Remember, **"Nothing is impossible for God."**

Don't be afraid of death so much as an inadequate life.
—Bertolt Brecht

Chapter 11
The Highest Mandate

The Great Commission was to make disciples of all nations, not just individuals. The Lord said that when He returned He would divide the nations into "sheep" or "goats." The sheep are good and the goats are bad. We have come to a time when nations are determining ultimate issues that will result in them being a sheep or goat nation.

I will continue to unpack the dream I had about the American Republic that deals with ultimate issues of our purpose from heaven's perspective. Regardless of what country you are from, there will be a level of civil conflict coming in your nation too. Many will be similar to what is unfolding in America. Therefore, even though this is American-centric, in many ways it addresses the same basic issues all nations will be facing, as these are all connected to what The Lord said would come at the end of this age.

As covered previously, the first two Great Awakenings in America each preceded wars—the Revolutionary War and the Civil War. As we study the primary messages that came from those two Great Awakenings, we can see a direct link from the Awakenings to the wars. Did these great spiritual awakenings cause the wars? In some basic ways they did. The light from these Awakenings exposed the darkness, and this required that it be confronted until it was driven from the land. When this was not done spiritually then the physical conflict became inevitable.

Could the darkness have been driven from the land by spiritual warfare so that the physical conflicts would not have been necessary? Yes. That is almost always the case, and of course that certainly would have been desirable. However, what I saw in my dream included physical conflict. I saw the nature of this, which I will share later in this study. Even so, it is my conviction that to the degree that evil strongholds in our land are destroyed spiritually, the degree of the physical conflict will be reduced.

As we enter the Third Great Awakening in America, we can expect the same kind of light to expose the great darkness in our time. When powers of darkness are exposed, they rage. When they are cast out of their high positions they come to the earth with great wrath, as we see in Revelation 12. God's provision is to send us great champions of the truth to face specific evil strongholds in our time. They are being sent to completely destroy these strongholds, not just defeat them and push them back. What is happening in the Spirit will be reflected in the natural with rage and conflict.

It is always a tragedy when our differences degenerate into violence. It has been a great hope of Western Civilization to rise above war, to eradicate it completely from the earth. That is a noble hope, however, as we see up to the end of the Book of Revelation, there will be increasing war right to the end of the age.

As we see in Revelation 7, for a brief time the winds of war (winds of the earth) are held back so that The Lord's bondservants can be sealed, but this is a short time and the winds are released again. To be prepared for the times we must understand that violence has already begun, and it will get worse for a time. Again, this may be reduced by spiritual victories, but there is now a level of violence that we will not be able to avoid and we must be prepared for—spiritually and physically.

A major reason we can expect increasing violence is because of a contingent that not only does not want open debate, but cannot tolerate it. This is the fruit of an education system that no longer educates, but indoctrinates. A generation has been conditioned so that if you disagree with them they will be offended, and being offended has been elevated to the level of being considered almost worse than a physical assault. That many are so easily offended is a major cause that will make the physical violence unavoidable. As we are told in Proverbs 18:19, **"A brother offended is harder to be won than a strong city."**

We cannot compromise the truth in order not to offend people. Even Jesus declared that He was "a rock of offense, and a stone to stumble over." There is not one thing that Jesus did that is recorded in the Gospels that He was not criticized for or threatened for. If we follow Him we can expect the same, and if we are not being persecuted it can reflect the level of compromise that we have allowed in our life.

This being understood, one of the most important things we can do to prepare for the coming conflict is to refuse to be offended. This is basic Christianity and is called "forgiveness." Jesus forgave the ones who had Him crucified and even those who nailed Him to the cross. Learning to be quick to forgive is basic discipleship and basic to following Christ. To stay on the right side in what is unfolding, we must not engage in the rage and bitterness that is fueled by unforgiveness. We must learn not to react to personal offense, but take the actions that we do because they are the right thing to do.

To make it through what is coming upon the world will require all Christians to follow Christ more closely and be more like Him than we ever have. We must guard our hearts, especially from the evil stronghold of unforgiveness and offense.

The Lord will help us get ready by allowing opportunities to learn to forgive quickly and totally.

Don't waste these trials. Embrace them as the opportunities they are, especially when you are persecuted for doing what is right. The Lord promised a special blessing for this. See these as an opportunity to get closer to The Lord by bearing your cross to identify with Him, and getting closer to Him will be the greatest blessing of all.

People living deeply have no fear of death. –*Anais Nin*

Chapter 12

No Victory Without a Battle

One of the biggest evil strongholds now growing in the U.S. is causing people to be offended by just about anything. The penalty for causing someone to be offended is getting increasingly severe and has even been proposed to be a criminal offense, just as it has already become in many Western countries. This has led to people being increasingly controlled by the fear of offending someone to the point of almost completely shackling free expression. This is a basic assault on one of the two linchpin freedoms that all of our other freedoms stand on—the freedom of speech.

This has led to another growing bondage in our land—the "tyranny of the minority." This is how a tiny percentage of people can claim to be offended by something and by this take away the rights of everyone else. This is how prayer was taken out of our public schools, which fueled the assault on just about every other religious expression. This was a very basic violation of The Constitution that has led to its continued demise.

Led by the increasingly dominant thought police, lawmakers and judges have sided with this basic and final assault on our freedom. They are now even proposing that almost anything that is contrary to liberal political correctness is "hate speech" deserving of criminal prosecution and punishment. If this is accomplished it will mean the complete demise of our Republic and our liberty.

A law was proposed in the European Union recently that would make it a crime to even criticize E.U. immigration policy. There have been even more onerous laws proposed in the United Nations that would have been binding on all member nations, except the Muslim nations, Russia, and China. Go figure. It hasn't happened yet, but that is just one step away from making it a crime to criticize any policy, which is just one step away from the release of a worldwide Gestapo.

We may think that America would never fall that far, but we have tended to only be a few steps behind such trends in Europe. However, the American Republic is not going to fall that far, not because we are so much smarter or stronger, but because of the grace of God. A major pushback is coming against all of the PC madness that has sought to bind and micro-manage people until they are compliant automatons.

In II Corinthians 3:17, we are told that **"where the Spirit of the Lord is, there is liberty."** The subjugation of the people is always an attempt to hinder the moving of The Spirit of The Lord. The spirit behind the PC madness and the subsequent laws is an attempt to inhibit the coming greatest move of God that there has ever been.

It is now easy to see the factors that are causing the internal social pressures to increase until they explode. A major factor that we need to see and address is how the church is responsible for this. What we release in heaven, or from our spiritual position, gets released on the earth. What we bind in the spiritual we've been called to will get bound on the earth. Is this basic intolerance of freedom of speech or freedom of thought not dominant in most of the church?

The seeds of intolerance now expanding in the world were sown by the Pharisaical spirit in much of the church. Even with the great movements that were born out of a revelation that recovered and restored biblical truth to the church, almost all quickly became intolerant of any who did not agree with them, or presumed to go even further than they had in the pursuit of the truth. That is the spirit that operated in the Pharisees, not Jesus.

This is not to imply that we should let anyone teach anything in the church. We must have a devotion to adhering to sound biblical teaching, but we must do this because we love the truth, not because we are threatened by those who see some things differently. The spirit of intolerance is evil regardless of where it is found. The counter to this spirit is not tolerance of anything, but rather a love for the truth that defends and protects the truth in the Spirit of Christ.

The church is responsible for allowing many evils to be released into these times by what we have tolerated. Even so, the church will also be the source of what breaks the power of this evil. A new revolution is coming to the church, and then through it. The result of this will be the release of great champions of the truth that will be some of the most powerful messengers to walk the earth.

As we see in Revelation 12, when Satan is cast out of heaven, or the high positions he controls, he will come to the earth with great wrath. Because Satan dwells in darkness, just his exposure by the light begins to break his power, and he will react to the coming light with all of the violence he can muster. There are now many conditioned reactionaries who will come in great violence who must not be confused with the righteous revolutionaries.

Presently, most of our divisions have been cast in political terms, either liberal or conservative. There are other alternatives to these two. There is a transcendent truth, a transcendent cause that is beyond politics, and it will ultimately prevail. Just as a basic military strategy is to take the high ground and fight from it, we must do the same. We must not get pulled down into the low ground of lesser issues.

The unhappy person resents it when you try to cheer him up, because that means he has to stop dwelling on himself and start paying attention to the universe. Unhappiness is the ultimate form of self-indulgence. *–Tom Robbins*

Be happy. It's one way of being wise. *–Colette*

The joy of the Lord is our strength. *–Nehemiah*

Chapter 13
Seeing

It is basic military doctrine that you cannot defeat an enemy you do not see. Seeing the enemy implies understanding him. Just as the most effective military leaders are those who learn the ways of their adversaries so they can counter them, we are commanded not to be ignorant of the enemy's schemes.

After studying our nation's founding and being convinced that the hand of God was in it and that our founding documents were inspired by wisdom from above, it was easy to see how the enemy would seek to destroy us and thereby destroy God's purpose for our nation. In my dream, I saw one word in large caps that summed up our purpose: LIBERTY. This was followed by *"and justice for all."* We cannot have true liberty if it is not for all, and we cannot have true justice unless it is for all.

One of the primary linchpins holding our Constitution together has been under relentless assault by the enemies of our freedom. This assault has come primarily through the courts by activist judges. Their ultimate target has been to eradicate religious liberty. Their main strategy has been to set us adrift by a false interpretation of the relationship between the church and the state established in The Constitution.

It is very possible that not all of these judges knew the impact of their decisions and how they were an assault on our Constitution and therefore our Republic. Just as Jesus prayed for those who crucified Him to be forgiven because they did not know what they were doing, this is often the case with those used by the devil. This is why we are told that we do not war against flesh and blood, but against the principalities and powers using people to do their work. Even so, we must see the strategy to counter it.

Nowhere in The Constitution is there mention of the separation of the church and state. This is a major fallacy and deception by which the enemies of the truth have worked to destroy a linchpin of our Republic—the freedom of religion. Most Americans, and even many conservatives who promote adherence to The Constitution, believe this lie that The Constitution mandated a separation of church and state. What is actually stated is that *"congress will establish no religion, or prohibit the free exercise thereof."* This was intended to keep the federal government out of the church, not the other way around. The Founders even argued that the Republic could not last without the influence of religion.

Again, the term "separation of church and state" is not found in The Constitution or any other founding documents. Those who say that it is are only revealing their ignorance of The Constitution. This term was coined by Thomas Jefferson in his letters to the Danbury Baptists. That term, and his letters, were intended to ensure them that the church would be protected from the intrusion of the state, not the other way around.

This false interpretation of The Constitution and its wrong application has resulted in the attempt to use the government, especially the courts, to inhibit the freedom of religion in America. This is itself a serious violation of The Constitution and Bill of Rights. This must be resisted until this lie is broken off of our land.

We can see that in the year this began to be wrongly applied by the Supreme Court to remove prayer from public schools,

America began its present meltdown in morality, righteousness, and justice. By this decision the Supreme Court allowed a tiny fraction of the population that were atheists and agnostics to sever one of the most basic and important provisions of The Constitution and violate the religious liberty of the rest of the country.

For this to be allowed to stand—and the way that it was done through the Supreme Court without even being contested— has led to the eroding of many other basic liberties, and now has our continued existence as a Republic in jeopardy. It did this by allowing the judicial tyranny to go to a new level of intrusion on the authority of the other branches of government, the states, and the people.

As application of Supreme Court decisions have become even more intrusive into the rights reserved to the states and the people, it has brought us to the crisis point where it will be determined if we live or die as a Republic. To be the salt and light that Christians are called to be, we must resolve to stand against evil, injustice, and tyranny. We are called to be "freedom fighters" and it should be fundamental to all Christians to fight for "liberty and justice for all."

Stewardship is one of the basic ways we will be judged as faithful or unfaithful to The Lord, as Jesus explained in the Parable of the Talents. This is not just about stewarding our money or stuff, but also stewarding all that God has entrusted to us. As Americans we must be good stewards of the freedoms that have been entrusted to us and the light that our Constitution has been to the world, but we have allowed it to be removed from our own land.

The only commandment that God gave with a promise attached is to honor our fathers and mothers. The promise given for doing this is that it would "go well" with us and that our days would be prolonged. What could be more dishonoring of our national fathers and mothers than to lose what was entrusted to us on our watch, which was paid for by such a dear price? America has been called "the home of the brave," and we have been preserved by the courage and sacrifice of many. Now it is our turn.

Courage is the greatest need we have today in our Christian and national leadership. When the first apostles were threatened by the Sanhedrin they did not pray for more wisdom, protection, or even more power—they prayed for boldness. Boldness is the fruit of courage. We are about to see a bold new breed of leader arise.

Happiness is when what you think, what you say, and what you do are in harmony. –*Gandhi*

Chapter 14
Justice

In the last chapter we covered how the reversing of what our Constitution said about the relationship between church and state led to increased stifling of not just all religious liberty, but even our freedom of speech. This led to the erosion of morality and integrity, as well as our other liberties and The Constitution's authority itself.

Using the courts to do this was a main strategy of the enemies of liberty, using them to exercise a power they do not have under The Constitution—the power to legislate new law. They have accomplished this to such a degree they are now close to being able to almost completely nullify the power of our Constitution.

Judges are human; we cannot expect them to be perfect. We will not have a perfect judicial system on earth until the kingdom comes. But it is easily arguable that America has had the best system of justice in history, until recently.

An assault on America's religious liberty may not have been the intent of the judges issuing the judgments that led to this, but it was the effect. That's why the Founders in The Constitution gave Congress, not the judicial branch, the authority to keep the government moored to The Constitution. When Congress allowed their authority in this to be usurped by the judicial, everything the Founders foresaw as the greatest threat to our Republic—judicial tyranny—came upon us.

As shocking as this thought may be to most Americans, the judicial branch was not given the authority to determine what was constitutional or unconstitutional, and for a very good reason. Federal judges, and even Supreme Court Justices, are not elected and therefore do not answer to the people for their decisions. This authority was given to the Congress because it was believed that in Congress, free and open debate would be required for congressional action. Therefore, Congress would be more likely to come to the right interpretation of The Constitution, the supreme law of the land. This was more likely than putting such weighty decisions in the hands of a single judge, or even small groups of them such as the Supreme Court.

Again, the Supreme Court does not have the authority to interpret any law as being constitutional or unconstitutional unless this is asked of them by Congress. It was asked of them early in our history on an issue Congress considered itself too busy to research and address at the time, and the Supreme Court has assumed this authority since. That this was allowed has proven catastrophic by leading to increasing judicial tyranny. It has also led to the increasing and unnecessarily vicious conflicts among the people over issues that were designated as authority reserved for the states and the people, and for a good reason. No small body of unelected judges or justices were to be allowed to impose their will, or their interpretation of major issues, on the whole country.

So, what is the Supreme Court for? First, it was probably misnamed "the Supreme Court" because this could so easily be interpreted as the ultimate arbiter of the law and The Constitution, a place it now wrongly assumes. What it was meant to be was the final court of appeals, and probably should have been named "high court" rather than Supreme Court.

You can have the best form of government and still have bad government if you do not have good people in it. Our Republic has not failed, but we have failed the Republic. The present growing crisis could have been avoided if we had honored our national fathers by heeding their warnings, especially about the threat of judicial tyranny.

Because judges are now so politicized, making decisions based more on political prejudices or expediency rather than the merits of each case or its adherence to The Constitution, increasingly desperate political maneuvering now dominates the judicial branch. For there to be true justice, no politics should be allowed in the judicial, but we have now drifted far from that.

A strong, just, independent judiciary is necessary for true justice. This can only be recovered and maintained by strong, just, independent judges who are committed to staying in their lane as established by The Constitution. For any judge to legislate from the bench, or make law, is unconstitutional. Congress alone was given the authority to make laws, not the judiciary or executive branches.

Weak, inept leadership in Congress has allowed its authority to be usurped by both the judicial and executive branches. Every time this is allowed and goes uncontested by Congress, The Constitution's authority as the supreme law of the land is weakened, and we continue spiraling down toward a terrible chaos. Later we will address specific examples of when and how this happened and the damage it has done, but there is another culprit in this we must address first—the church.

Again, whenever we see major destructive strongholds growing in our land we need to look at the church first because what we release or bind in heaven gets released, or bound, on the earth—or our salt has lost its ability to preserve and our light has not been shining. In the next chapter, we will examine the connection between the failure of church leadership and the release of judicial tyranny in our land.

For one human being to love another human being: that is perhaps the most difficult task that has been entrusted to us, the ultimate task, the final test and proof, the work for which all other work is merely preparation. *—Rainer Maria Rilke*

Chapter 15

Judicial Tyranny in the Church

In the last chapter we began to discuss the link between the judicial tyranny threatening our Republic and how the church has been a culprit in this. We need to understand this if this evil is to be eradicated from the roots.

In Matthew 16, Jesus asked His disciples who men say that He is. This is the dialogue that followed in Matthew 16:16-19:

Simon Peter answered, "You are the Christ, the Son of the living God."

And Jesus said to him, "Blessed are you, Simon Barjona, because flesh and blood did not reveal this to you, but My Father who is in heaven.

"I also say to you that you are Peter, and upon this rock I will build My church; and the gates of Hades will not overpower it.

"I will give you the keys of the kingdom of heaven; and whatever you bind on earth shall have been bound in heaven, and whatever you loose on earth shall have been loosed in heaven."

The "rock" that The Lord is building His church on is not Peter, which means "a little stone," but rather the rock that is The Father's revelation of who Jesus is. No one is part of His true church because they have parents that knew The Lord, or sit under a pastor that does. We must each have our own revelation from The Father of who Jesus is. That is the "rock" the church is built upon—that all of God's people will know Him for themselves.

Then Jesus states the authority of this church to prevail over the gates of hell, what is bound on earth gets bound in heaven, and what is loosed on earth gets loosed in heaven. Heaven is not just the next life—it is a term often used as a reference to the spiritual realm. This is a statement about the remarkable and yet rarely understood and untapped authority given to the church that what it releases in the spirit will be pervasive on earth. When we understand the prevalence of the spiritual realm over the earth, we understand its influence over the affairs of mankind.

So how might this apply with regard to our government, Constitution, and the judicial tyranny that our Founding Fathers warned would be the greatest threat to the Republic? In I Corinthians 6, the Apostle Paul lamented that there were no judges in the church in Corinth. They were called to "judge angels," but it was to their shame that they could not find a single one wise enough to judge the small matters of this life. Now let us consider, is there a church anywhere where such wise judges can be found?

New Testament church government was modeled after the Old Testament government Moses established for Israel and was carried over into the Promised Land. In this model, elders sat in the gates of cities to judge the people, hearing and deciding disputes and even carrying out judicial duties, such as authenticating deeds. The elders established in the New Testament churches were likewise expected to be the judges of the congregations they served. Paul lamented to the Corinthian church that their elders were not doing this. When he said that this was "to their shame," he was likely being far more prophetic than he may have realized, as this lack could be attributed to most of the shame that the body of Christ has suffered to this day.

In Psalm 89:14 we are told that righteousness and justice are the foundations of The Lord's throne, which is His authority. Righteousness and justice go together—you cannot have one without the other. If we are called to judge angels, how is it possible that we do not have such justice in the church? Why is the world not beating a path to our door seeking our wisdom for justice? It does not do this because the church might be the last place they think of as having the wisdom of just and righteous judges. We have strayed that far.

Now there are many false teachings circulating in the church about God's judgment, not to mention our calling to have righteous and wise judges in the church. So, the result is basically judicial tyranny in the church where those with control spirits dominate. Or we have anarchy in the church where elders are afraid to judge anything. Do we not have the same in our country? We have those presuming and usurping authority that do not legally have to impose their own opinions and prejudices on the land, or we have those who literally let murderers get away with it.

What is the solution? First, we need sound teaching on the judgment of God, the Judgment Seat of Christ—the authority that leaders in the church such as elders have "to judge those who are in the church," as the Apostle Paul asserted. Since judicial tyranny and judicial anarchy are now the greatest threats to our country, the church that is called to be the light of this world should have answers to these ultimate issues with a righteous devotion to justice that even the world would start to desire.

Righteousness is doing what is right in the sight of The Lord. Justice is basically about people being treated fairly, and The Lord cares deeply about that. Both of these are key factors if we are going to build our houses on the rock and stand against the storms.

You learn to speak by speaking, to study by studying, to run by running, to work by working; in just the same way, you learn to love by loving. *–Saint Francis de Sales*

Chapter 16

Strength Made Perfect In Weakness

As we began to address in the last two chapters, much of the responsibility for the increasing darkness in our times belongs to the church—our failing to be the light that we are called to be. While there are many great churches today, overall the church in America may be the weakest it has ever been. We cannot blame politicians for the failure of the American Republic without also blaming ourselves for failing to be the salt and light we are called to be.

In examining the failures of both the church and our government, we are not trying to find someone to blame; rather, we are seeking to understand the problems so we can know the solutions, and how they too are connected to one another.

We can see the American Republic's failure to adhere to The Constitution as a reflection of how the church failed to adhere to the supreme authority of The Scriptures. We see the failure of the American Republic to be a nation where all men are treated equally as a reflection of the spiritual bigotry in the church. This is not just racism (though that is a major problem in the church), but religious bigotry. Religious bigotry is believing ourselves to be better than others because we are part of a certain denomination or movement. It is the same evil of judging by externals rather than by the Spirit.

The plague of abortion is a reflection of how the church has aborted many of the seeds that God planted in it to bring forth new missions, ministries, and spiritual generations, but the church aborted these seeds. The church usually aborts them for the same reasons that millions of children have their lives snuffed out by their physical mothers—because they come at an inconvenient time, they are expensive, or we are too busy for them. Has the church not been just as selfish?

The increasing domination of the culture by the homosexual agenda is a reflection of the church's spiritual homo-sect-uality, which is having relations with your own kind. We were made different to have interchange and to learn how much we need each other, not to separate from the rest of the body. The Creator loves diversity so much He made each one of us different, and His unity is a unity of diversity, not a unity of conformity. So, where does this pressure to conform in the church come from?

The rising addiction to drugs in America is a reflection of how the church has exchanged the life of sacrifice and taking up our cross to a "feel good faith" that only teaches and practices what will make the people feel good. Pain is not a bad thing. It is a messenger to tell us that something is wrong. When we seek to avoid the pain without seeking to understand why it is there, we allow something wrong to continue and the problems to get worse. When we embrace the cross and take it up daily, we learn to face the pain and remove it by dealing with the cause.

We could go on with this list, but we must not blame the heathen for being heathen—they are only doing what we would be doing if we had not been shown grace. Instead of being quick to condemn our government leaders for departing from The Constitution, let us search our own hearts and ask The Holy

Spirit to convict us of our sin where we have departed from the ways He made so clear in His Word. We must humble ourselves and pray, seeking His face and turning from our wicked ways. If we will do this, He has promised to heal our land.

We must rise up to resist the evil that is destroying us and our land, but we must keep a humble, repentant heart, not thinking of ourselves as superior to those who have fallen lest we have the grace by which we stand removed. We must be quick to show grace to others when they repent, just as we have been shown grace. Pointing out any who have failed to adhere to the Word of God or The Constitution it is not to condemn, but it is so the gate of hell through which the evil has come into the church and our country is shut.

That the church in America is at such a lowly state can ultimately work for our good if it keeps us humble, since God gives His grace to the humble. The Lord had seemingly endless grace for repentant sinners, but He had none for the self-righteous. We need to keep in mind that the church that fell to such a low state happened on our watch.

For this reason, let us resolve that this will not be the end of our story. Let us be counted with those who in the darkest of times throughout history turned the hearts of the people back to The Lord and helped deliver them from their oppressors.

The things you own end up owning you. *–Chuck Palahniuk*

Stop accumulating stuff, and start accumulating experiences. *–James Wallman*

Chapter 17
A New Beginning

The church as we perceive it in the West is about to die. This is to rejoice over. This is not to imply that the church in the West has not accomplished many great things, but it is time to move on. Even though it may yet be far from what the church is intended to be, and will be, it has accomplished much and will die in honor.

This is a parallel of the life of Rachel, Jacob's wife that died when Benjamin was born. Benjamin was the last son born to Israel and represents the last sons of God to be born on the earth. Benjamin means "the son of the right hand," and the right hand of God is called "the right hand of power." Like Rachel, the church will give birth to the "son of His right hand," but it will take her life. This means she will have been a mother to the last-day ministry, and we honor our fathers and mothers.

The Reformation helped the church dig its way out of the deep darkness of the Dark Ages. As far as Christianity has advanced over the last five hundred years, we yet have much further to go. This does not mean it will take another five hundred years. As we are told in II Peter 3:8, **"But do not let this one fact escape your notice, beloved, that with the Lord one day is like a thousand years, and a thousand years like one day."** This means He can do in one day what we think will take a thousand years.

What will happen will not happen through the continued reformation of the present model of the church, but through a revolution. There is a new breed of ministry about to be released. It will be composed of people who walk in radical, revolutionary faith and power. This is such a new wine that the old model cannot contain it. For this reason, we should not despair when the old model dies, but rightfully honor the Rachel that carried and gave birth to the new breed. But it is time for a new breed to come forth.

Likewise, a new breed of radical, revolutionary patriots will arise in America, and not just America—in nations around the world. God established the nations and gave them boundaries. He said anyone who moved the ancient boundaries would be cursed. That's because He wants the nations preserved. Again, God's unity is a unity of diversity, not a unity of conformity that earthly men are trying to impose on the world through globalism. God's unity will prevail, and patriotism is going to win around the world. In this way the heritage and inheritances will be preserved, national and cultural identities will be preserved, and the great unity of diversity will become manifest.

Once we see our purpose, we can see how the church in America has deviated from its calling and see how the same thing has happened in our civil government. "We the people" are the ones that are primarily responsible for this because the people are the sovereign. The government of the Republic is designed to be subject to the people, not the other way around. The primary blame for having our authority usurped lies ultimately with us for allowing it to happen. The people will also be the ones who wake up and recover what has been lost.

This is a prophecy of what is coming, but it is also a forensic study of what went wrong so that we can correct it, and stop making the same mistakes that have been so devasting to the church and the world that the church is supposed to be the light of. If we do not understand the mistakes, we will fall again because what caused the fall has not been corrected. Just as Spurgeon once said that he could find ten men who would die for The Bible for every one that would read it, we too can find many who would die for The Constitution who have obviously not even read it.

As I shared before, our ministry lawyer took Constitutional Law in law school and they never once referred to The Constitution. The entire course was spent studying Supreme Court decisions, obviously under the delusion that the Supreme Court was the supreme law of the land and that anything it would do must be constitutional. Much of what they did was in fact contrary to The Constitution and eroded its authority as the "supreme law of the land." Those who claim to be "constitutional lawyers" can be the most ignorant of what is actually in The Constitution. When a politician today says that something is constitutional, you can almost be sure that it is not. When they claim that something is not constitutional, you can almost be sure that it is.

That is how twisted things have become and why The Lord's first warning about these times was, **"Do not be deceived."** Deception is far more common than truth today. This is why things reported in the media are now more likely to be false, or at least distorted. How have we come to such a low place? You can now count on the same from what is coming from most of the pulpits in the American church. The message of the typical American church today would be unrecognizable to the apostles of the first century. Not so for what is coming.

The disconnect from truth has come the same way in the media that it has in the church. Of course, this is not true in every church or every media. It's easy to see in the media how there is now a tendency to report what they want to be true rather than what is true. Is that not how we have changed the Gospel, the church, and even our concept of God into what we want them to be rather than how they are?

One of the basic characteristics of true humility is being teachable and responsive enough to accept correction, and then to change our concepts and beliefs. This is repentance, and a great move of repentance is coming. Just as repentance had to be preached to prepare for The Lord's first coming, the same is true for His second coming.

It's not what happens to you, but how you react to it that matters. –*Epictetus*

Chapter 18

Correct or Politically Correct

Jesus had to be the most un-politically correct person to ever walk the earth. The more we become like Him, the more we will be too. He did not fear men. He was not running for office or seeking to win a popularity contest. He came to tell us the truth. This too will be the nature of the new breed of ministry about to be released.

Politics is built on human alliances and humanly devised methods and strategies. These can be good and effective, but they can never measure up to obedience to God. Politics now dominates the church in America, and true spiritual leadership that is based on following The Lord is rare. The religious spirit has more influence than The Holy Spirit in most of the church today. The counterfeit authority of manipulation, control, and hype are substituted for the true spiritual authority that comes from following The King.

Paul wrote in Galatians 1:10 that if he was still seeking to please men he would not be a bondservant of Christ. There is nothing more corrupting of true authority than the fear of man, being a respecter of persons, or what we today call politics. This is a primary reason why the church can now be the last place that we can find God, and why the government can be the last place that we find true authority, statesmanship, or wisdom.

What can we expect from our leaders in the church when we have made hirelings out of them—being more dependent on men than God? This modern model for ministry is a perversion of what the ministry is called to be.

Likewise, our Republic was not designed to be run by professional politicians, but rather by servant leaders who go to Congress like one goes to jury duty. In the beginning, there were few benefits to serving in government. One did it for their country, and often at great sacrifice. That model of representation will again be restored in our Republic. It must or it too will not survive just like the archaic model of church leadership.

Both professional politicians and professional ministers are two species that need to be extinct. They will be when real leaders and true ministers emerge. Obviously, this calls for radical change in both the church and the government. Neither will survive much longer without such radical change. In both cases the death of the old is required so that the new can emerge.

So how do we do this? The first step is simple, although this does not mean it is easy. We must go back to our founding documents—The Bible and The Constitution. Then we must resolve to comply with and defend them against those who would bend or dilute them. We must resolve to no longer follow false leaders or false shepherds.

The Supreme Court is not the supreme law of the land—The Constitution is. Many Supreme Court decisions are contrary to The Constitution. Possibly no other entity is more responsible than the Supreme Court for the severing of our government's ties to The Constitution. Likewise, the same could be said for the modern model of church leadership.

A best-case scenario would be if the Supreme Court realized its departure from The Constitution, began to own the discord this caused in the country, and then initiate the necessary corrections. This would begin to quickly diffuse much of the discord in our country, help restore The Constitution's authority, and restore respect for government. This action would have many consequences in our country, virtually all of them good. It would likely raise the stature and make heroes out of the Supreme Court, instead of the goat it will become if it does not do this.

This could also go a long way to restoring justice in the country, which requires the non-political nature of the judicial. It would likewise force the other branches of government to examine their own deviation from The Constitution and correct it. This would be a best-case scenario—to have the branch of government most responsible for the biggest threats to our continued existence as a Republic wake up and take action to reverse them. That should be our prayer. If only one or two justices awoke to this and stood up to defend The Constitution as they swore to do, it could ignite a movement that gets this done.

The next best-case scenario would be for the legislative branch to awaken to its constitutional authority and responsibility and rein in the judicial and executive branches from their overreach, as they were given the authority to do. They were the only branch of government given the power of impeachment and the purse in order to do this.

Of course, the legislative branch has its own sins to repent of, but this would certainly turn around their present single digit approval rating and help restore faith in the government. This will take extraordinary leadership with extraordinary courage, but extraordinary leadership is from God when it comes, and nothing is impossible for Him. We must appeal to Him for leaders who are after His heart and live to do His will.

The next best-case scenario would be for a President to grasp the departure we have made from The Constitution, and for him or her to use the exceptional power of that office's "bully pulpit" to give a clear trumpet call for the repentance and restoration needed.

The illumination of how far our government has deviated from our constitutional moorings is coming, it is certain and the reform is coming. How hard and how costly the struggle is to do this depends on us. In Psalm 115:16 we are told, **"The heavens are the heavens of the Lord, but the earth He has given to the sons of men."** This is why The Lord will not do things on the earth until we pray. He delegated authority over the earth to men, and "the gifts and callings of God are without repentance" (see Romans 11:29)—He does not take them back.

Those who illuminate it, initiate it, and follow through on getting it done for our government will deserve to be esteemed as a new generation of Founders. That will be a great honor. As we see in Isaiah 58, it will be one of the great honors to be **"a repairer of the breech, a restorer of the streets in which to dwell" (see Isaiah 58:12)**. To be this for our civil government will be an honor for the ages, but how much more so will it be to have been a restorer of the house of The Lord? Someone is going to do this; why not us?

I never saw a wild thing sorry for itself. A small bird will drop frozen dead from a bough without ever having felt sorry for itself. –D.H. Lawrence

Chapter 19

Leaders of the New Revolution

In the last chapter we discussed scenarios of how the needed corrections to our government could come from within the government, starting with the three branches of the federal government. In this chapter we will look at what could be done if that does not happen.

The next best alternative would be for state government leaders to awaken to what has been done to our Republic, and a movement begun to recover their authority that was usurped by the federal government. The federal government was created by the states, not the other way around. Under The Constitution, the only authority that the federal government has is what is specified in The Constitution, which was limited by intent. All other authority remained with the states and the people. This must be recovered.

There could also be a combination of leaders from the different branches of the federal government who join with state leaders to save the Republic. That would take some of the greatest leadership since the Founders, if not even greater. Since good leadership is a blessing from God, we should not count that out just because there does not seem to be such leadership on the radar at this time. We must appeal to God. He hears us and wants to respond to the prayers that are according to His will.

I have known many who were great leaders with courage and wisdom who ran for office and went to Washington. It was not long before they could only think politically, not as the leaders they once were. The beast that our federal government has become seems to devour most who come to it. Right now, there is little reason to think our dysfunctional government can make the dramatic but necessary corrections on its own; however, there are some in it who have maintained their integrity. Some of the most revolutionary tipping points in history came through a tiny percentage of the people. There are more than enough in our government now, on all levels, to get this done.

If the government does not soon begin its own radical reformation, the people will do it. This will be another Revolution/Civil War, and that is where we are headed. I was given a vivid revelation of how this would happen several years ago, but I did not realize what I was seeing at the time, and that it applied to us. Now I do. Like the patriots in our first revolution, this is a job too big for any men, and they knew it would never happen without God's intervention. He intervened for our founding, and He will intervene again for our preservation. Our faith must be in Him and not ourselves, but we must do our part for Him to do His. The Holy Spirit is the Helper, not the Doer.

As painful, costly, and destructive as it will be if our government leaders do not bring the needed restoration, for the people to do it would be the most effective way to restore the Republic and set our course toward fulfilling our destiny. Many of "the people" who do this will be the wealthiest and most successful, just as it was in the first revolution. Some who do the greatest exploits will come from the lowest, just as it was in the first revolution. We all have a part in this, and we must each know and do our part.

We also need to address some important questions, such as how to have another Revolution/Civil War without it fueling the anarchy and lawlessness that is growing so fast, or succumbing to the same political spirit that seems to devour anyone who exercises civil authority in these times. This does not seem humanly possible, so we are again cast in dependence upon God, which seems to be His intent. Wasn't this the case with the Founders?

The scattered and divided colonies had no earthly chance in taking on the most powerful empire in the world at the time. This simply was not possible without God, and it will not be possible to restore our Republic without Him. We need to remember that. We also need to remember that He seldom moves on our behalf until it is impossible for us. We must get used to facing impossible situations, and resolving to live by faith that nothing is impossible for God.

Yet, God uses people to do His work. Friends have commented that we need another George Washington. I personally think we will need a combination of Washington, Lincoln, Moses, and maybe the Apostle Paul. Even Washington needed the great company of remarkable leaders that the rest of the Founders were. Where are those of such a stature today that could pull off something like this? They are likely in the same place they were in 1775—hidden from everyone, including themselves, until the fullness of time came.

Regardless of how confusing and hard things may get, never forget that fixing our little issues here would be a very easy thing for the One who upholds the universe with His power. He seems to have wanted us to come to the place where there is just no way we can be saved without Him. There really never is, but there are some situations where it is more obvious than others, such as the one we're now in. So, what is our part?

1. Obey II Chronicles 7:14.

2. Have faith in God.

3. Do our due diligence and get the education we need to discuss this with our circle of influence.

4. Resolve to stand for the truth with unyielding boldness as we are given the grace to see it.

5. Join with other groups or associations that are gathering to become educated and take action. Many are now engaged in such important things as contacting lawmakers, judges, and other officials to help educate them, or at least begin a dialogue.

6. Resolve to never give up, for the sake of our families, our fellow citizens, and all of those who risked their lives, or gave them, for the Republic we were given.

7. Always keep in mind that "the main thing is to keep the main thing the main thing." The main thing is loving God, His truth, and His people.

More will become clear as we get engaged. As the law of inertia teaches us, it is not possible to steer anything that is not moving. By getting engaged we are not likely to do everything perfectly, or even right, but if we start doing the best we know to do He can steer us toward the better way.

We are what we repeatedly do. Excellence, then is not an act, but a habit. –*Will Durant*

Chapter 20

You Are More Than You Know

"These are the times that try men's souls" (Thomas Paine). That is a good thing. James wrote that we should "count it all joy when you encounter various trails." Peter wrote that the test of our faith is more valuable than gold. So, if we have a biblical perspective we will get as excited by a new trial as we would if we had just found a bag of gold!

It will help us to navigate through these times if we understand that these times are meant to try us, because God considers us that valuable. The greatest prophets, the greatest souls, and the greatest leaders have always arisen during the darkest times. If we are alive for these times then we were made for them. God does not allow hard times to punish us, but rather to make us into what He has called us to be. He allows them because He loves us and thinks so highly of us that He is preparing us for leadership in His coming kingdom.

The Lord uses the title "Lord of hosts" over ten times more than all of His other titles. "Lord of hosts" means "Lord of armies." God refers to Himself as a Warrior. Yet we are told in Romans 16:20 that it is **"The God of Peace"** who crushes Satan under our feet. How is that?

The peace of God is not the freedom from conflict, but it is the confidence we have in God during the conflict. To see correctly through the storms, we must maintain that peace that comes from seeing Who is sitting on the throne *high* above all power and authority and dominion. Just as Peter walked on the waves as he kept his eyes on Jesus, but began to sink when he focused on the waves, we must see the waves to understand the times, but we do not focus on them. We must keep our focus on Jesus, and by this we can walk upon any troubled waters.

In this study, we are only looking superficially at how twisted and off track our federal government has become. Of course, this includes many state and local governments as well. There are other huge problems that we have not touched on, such as "the deep state." These too must be addressed and resolved if the government of the people will be restored. What we are facing is more than daunting, it is impossible— and we are probably in better shape than just about any other country! But here is an insight that may help you: it has been this way from the beginning of history. In fact, at times it has been much worse.

Since the fall, mankind has tottered on the edge of disaster. Almost every generation has fallen over the edge in some way, yet God made us so incredibly resourceful that we keep climbing out of the depths and somehow reach new heights. Then we tend to forget God who picked us back up, and we drift ever closer to the edge until we go over it again.

If we go through all that is coming in the Second American Revolution/Civil War—and we get our government back on the solid ground of following The Lord—could this happen again if The Lord tarries? It can. Read Israel's history in The Scriptures. It is a continuous cycle of The Lord blessing them with prosperity and peace, then they drift from The Lord and lose His hedge of protection. Then they are conquered, plundered, and enslaved by their enemies, until they cry out to God, He saves them, and it starts all over again.

So why spend all of our efforts and time for something that could just go awry again? First, we do it for The Lord. Then we do it for our families and our neighbors because it is the right thing to do. Not everyone will be good stewards, but we must resolve that we will do the best we can for God and His people while it is our time.

This life has been called "training for reigning." That is biblical. Since this is true, it will help if we keep our hope in the kingdom of God that will surely come. Then God's will is going to be done on earth as it is in heaven. This life is training to be part of His reign then, not just now. As we are told in Colossians 3:1-2, **"Therefore if you have been raised up with Christ, keep seeking the things above, where Christ is seated at the right hand of God. Set your mind on the things above, not on the things that are on earth."**

Therefore, we must resolve to fight the good fight and never quit, even when it looks like there is no hope of success in the natural. If it looks like there is no hope for success, it is because we are looking at the earthly instead of the heavenly. Our God who "stretched out the heavens like a tent curtain" (see Psalm 104:2) can fix every problem on earth so easily He would not even break a sweat if He took care of them all at once.

The ten evil spies did not think they could take the Promised Land because of how big the giants were. Joshua and Caleb didn't think the giants were a problem because they did not look at the size of the giants, or at their own size. Rather, they looked at the size of their God. We must do the same.

Always remember that "The main thing is to keep the main thing the main thing." The main thing that we are called to do is to love God. When that great judgment day comes, the main thing we will be judged on is how much we loved Him. We love His people and we love the nations because they are His inheritance, and we want Him to have the best inheritance from our nations as possible. We love the people because they are His children, and we want to do all that we can to see that His children are protected, provided for, and have the best possible government—one that truly is "for the people."

Paul wrote that he did all things for the sake of the Gospel (see I Corinthians 9:23). We do not preach the gospel of a political party, or of America, but of a much greater one that is coming. We are just working to prepare the way for it. This is how we do it.

The third-rate mind is only happy when it is thinking with the majority. The second-rate mind is only happy when it is thinking with the minority. The first-rate mind is only happy when it is thinking. –A.A. *Milne*

Chapter 21
From Darkness to Glory

In the first five chapters of Isaiah we see how Israel slipped away from its moorings to God and His covenant, falling into deeper and deeper corruption. Then they went beyond corruption to an ultimate depravity by calling good evil and evil good, honoring the dishonorable and dishonoring the honorable. How could any nation fall to such profound evil, much less one that had known The Lord the way Israel had and seen so many of His marvelous works on their behalf? The same way America now has.

America is now calling evil what God has called good and calling good what He has called evil. We dishonor the honorable, our remarkable national fathers and mothers, and honor the capricious, immature, and perverted. Like Israel suffered a number of times, America is now tottering on the brink of a terrible destruction.

God sought to turn back each step of Israel's fall with the discipline of His judgments. When they refused the message of His discipline, the judgments got more severe. In a final attempt to turn them back, the last judgment was to give them over to immature, capricious leaders. This was written about Israel, but it is a stunning parallel of what has now come upon America.

Some of the natural disasters prophesied to come upon nations to wake them up to their folly and turn them back to

The Lord are storms, floods, droughts, fires, and earthquakes. We have seen waves of these come, and each new wave has been more severe than the last. Just a few years ago it would have been alarming for the U.S. to spend $20 billion on natural disasters in a single year. In 2018, we spent almost a billion a day on them! That is correct, we spent over $300 billion dollars in one year on catastrophes that only insurance companies seem to have the understanding to call them what they are—"acts of God." How bad will it have to get before we repent?

The first step in restoring our Republic is to return to The Lord in repentance and humility. "We the people" must ultimately take ownership for the meltdown of the spiritual, moral, and constitutional foundations of our Republic. "We the people" must be responsible for restoring our moorings to the wisdom of government He gave to us, and the honoring of the honorable instead of the cowardly cow-towing to the most dishonorable among us now. If we return to The Lord by turning from our wicked ways and the depravity of calling "good evil, and evil good," He will return to us and give us mature, wise, godly leaders who will restore the Republic and lead us to fulfilling our destiny as a nation.

Why is having immature, capricious leaders the final judgment before destruction? We have all likely witnessed a family that has become subject to the tyranny of a five-year old. The spoiled, undisciplined child can dominate the entire family with their tantrums, determining where they go and what they do, or where they can't go and can't do. Now the U.S. is controlled to a large degree by a tiny percentage of the loudest, most obnoxious, and capricious among us. These demand tolerance for their aberrant behavior, yet they are the most intolerant of any who challenge them or resolve to be different.

When wise, decisive leadership is restored in a family, you can expect the tantrums to get even more severe for a time. Even so, if the family resolves not to endure the tyranny of the capricious five-year old, but holds their course, peace and order will be restored.

Peace and order can likewise be restored to our country, but we can expect some extreme outrage for a time when the capricious lose their influence. Much of what the country has been experiencing since 2016 is the result of authority beginning to be restored by a decisive President. As more authority and order come, we can expect more outrage from those who think they can control us by their tantrums, but peace and order is possible if we stay the course.

So, we have a choice. Are we going to continue to be controlled by the undisciplined and immature, or will a leadership arise that will not be controlled or manipulated, but rather persevere until order is restored? Either choice requires embracing some rough times ahead, but if we do what is right, things will ultimately get better. If we go the way of allowing the loudest, most obnoxious, and outrageous to control us, then we are headed for an increasing national nightmare.

We love the youth because parents tend to love their children more than they love their own lives. If we truly love the emerging generations, we will give attention to the biblical warnings for them. The Scriptures do not have anything good to say about the last generation. Both Jesus and the apostles described it as being deceived and prone to deception, because they can only hear what makes them feel good.

That is the nature of an immature, spoiled child, which biblical prophecies declare will result in them becoming **"disrespectful, irreconcilable, selfish, haters of good and lovers of evil" (II Timothy 3:3)**. What could better describe what the emerging generations are like now? This is not true of all, but it is of most. What can be done for them?

First, we must love them as The Scriptures exhort us to, which in Scripture is equated with discipline. King Solomon wrote that **"He who spares his rod hates his son" (see Proverbs 13:24)**. Contrary to biblical wisdom, child psychologists warned against spanking to the degree that it is now a crime in some countries and is treated like one here. Those psychologists promised that our tolerance and lack of discipline would produce wonderful, reasonable children. How has that worked out? It seems to have unleashed everything Jesus and the apostles warned about with the last generation.

However, we have this remarkable promise in Isaiah 60:1-5: When darkness is covering the earth and "deep darkness" the people, the glory of The Lord will arise and appear on His people. Then the nations will come to His Light! The Light will win! How does the Light win? It wins by the people turning back to it. It is time to turn back to biblical truth and turn away from the **"the wisdom that does not come from above, but is earthly, natural, and demonic" (see James 3:15)**.

The meeting of two personalities is like the contact of two chemical substances. If there is any reaction, both are transformed. –*Carl Jung*

Chapter 22
Getting Prepared

Before digging deeper into what is happening, and why it is leading to the Second American Revolution/Civil War, we will interject a few things that we must do immediately to be prepared for what is now unfolding.

The most important thing we can do to be positioned and prepared for what is unfolding is to find our place in The Lord's body, the church, and function in it. The longer we wait to do this, the more difficult it will be to do, and the consequences for not doing it soon will be greater. Knowing what is about to happen will not help us if we are not in the right place, doing what we were called and created to do.

The church is still far from what it is called to be. Great change is needed, and great change is coming. However, those who are waiting for the change to come before they try to be a part of it will be in danger of being in the company of the foolish virgins who waited too long. Those who will play an important role in His body need to be part of the process by which the body becomes what it is called to be.

To counter the spirit of this world that is bringing the darkness, we must move in an opposite spirit. We must resist the growing hatred by growing in love. We must resist the anxiety and fear by abiding in the peace of God and growing in faith. One of the primary ways we counter the spirit of division growing in the country is to grow in unity with The Lord and His people. It is not possible to be properly joined to The Lord and not also be joined to His body.

A basic requirement to grow in a spirit of unity is learning to resolve disputes in the right spirit. Church is one of the primary places we are called to learn this. Those who leave the church because they got offended are usually the same ones who end up leaving their marriages, jobs, and just about any other commitment when things don't go as they want. This is the symptom of the "spirit of divorce," or "spirit of division" that we are warned about in Scripture. We must resolve that we will not let that evil spirit rule our life and thereby ruin our life. We must also resolve that we will not let it rule our country and ruin it.

Divisions will come, as the Apostle Paul wrote to the Corinthians and the Apostle John wrote in I John 2. Sometimes divisions happen even between the best people, such as when Paul and Barnabas had a sharp conflict and parted ways. However, it is when there is a pattern of division that we must be concerned. This is an indication that one is operating in a "spirit of division." These are those that Jude addressed: **"In the last time there will be mockers, following after their own ungodly lusts. These are the ones who cause divisions, worldly-minded, devoid of the Spirit" (Jude 18-19)**.

I personally moved in this spirit of division the first few years I was a Christian. I caused many divisions and was guilty of slandering leaders and other Christians. I was often right about my evaluation of the problems, but moved in a spirit that brought division rather than being used by The Helper to fix problems. This was mostly because I was moving in a great amount of pride. My repentance started when I was shown that as I did unto the least of The Lord's little ones, I was doing it to

Him. I was then shown that what I was guilty of was far worse than anything those I criticized were guilty of.

There is a saying that "any jackass can kick a barn down, but it takes a skillful carpenter to build one." Have you ever known of a critic that started a revival? Have critics ever built anything of significance? Do you know of any who are celebrated in history? Many that The Scriptures call "fault-finders" will have accurate discernment and are right about the wrongs that they see, but they move in a foul spirit that only does harm to the work of God and His people. Jude reminds us that "the deep darkness" has been reserved for them. It would be much better to be wrong about a lot of things than to be a "fault-finder."

When Jesus saw what was wrong with the world He did not criticize or condemn us—He laid down His life for us. That will be the nature of the true leaders that He sends. As we are told in Ecclesiastes 3, there is a time for everything. There is a time to build and a time to tear down. The Apostle Paul said that he had the authority to build up or to tear down the Corinthian church. He had the authority to tear them down because he was the one used to plant and build them.

The point is that it is the builders who have the authority to tear down. It is the builders who have the heart for something, so they have the right heart to know what needs to be torn down. In the transformation that is coming, a lot will be torn down. There is a lot that needs to be torn down. However, we should not try to tear anything down without having a clear vision and a good plan for building what is to take its place.

The Apostle Paul wrote in Philippians 1:9, **"And this I pray, that your love may abound still more and more in real knowledge and all discernment."** **"Real knowledge"** and **"all discernment"** will only be found with the one whose love is abounding. For this reason, we will not have the knowledge or discernment that can help the church if we do not love it. Neither will we have the knowledge or discernment that helps our country if we do not love it.

We must not follow or even listen to critics, or fault-finders. If we do, we will become like them. We must learn to only follow and listen to builders who are leaving positive fruit from their works and their words.

He that cannot forgive others breaks the bridge over which he must pass himself, for every man has need to be forgiven. *–Edward Herbert*

Chapter 23
Treasure Hunters

In a world that is falling into increasing deception, we must be resolved to love the truth and to tell the truth without compromise. What makes something a treasure is that it is rare, or hard to get to. As integrity becomes increasingly rare, we must resolve that it is a treasure we will protect with the utmost diligence. One of the most important ways that we build our life on integrity is to obey what Jesus said in Matthew 5:37: **"But let your statement be, 'Yes, yes' or 'No, no'; anything beyond these is of evil."**

Contrary to His truth, children are often raised today by parents that don't really mean "yes" or "no" until they have repeated it many times and raised their voice to a certain decibel level. Or they teach their children that they can change the "yes" or "no" easily with a little pressure or manipulation. Jesus said this was "evil." By this we condition them to believe that we don't really mean what we say, and this carries on to them believing later that superiors at work or authorities don't really mean what they say. Worse, it has carried over so that to them The Lord does not really mean what He says, which is the trap that our first parents fell into and is at the root of most falls since.

This condition of not being able to hear or follow clear orders is getting increasingly costly, and sometimes deadly. In the military, to not hear and follow orders was a serious crime that drew severe punishment. This is because the potential cost is so high for anyone not to follow orders, putting many at risk—potentially the entire force, or even the nation they're defending. In the civilian sector, the penalty may not be that dramatic, but it is costly. It is also costly in relationships when one is found to be so undependable that they cannot be counted on to mean what they say.

This one thing is causing an increasing fracturing of our country. We don't believe our political leaders anymore because it's hard to believe anyone anymore. We don't believe the media. The courts are no longer trustworthy or consistent. Businesses are constantly caught in devious behavior, and universities are going insane. We are in the times described in Hebrews 12:27 when "everything that can be shaken will be shaken." What is the remedy?

Honesty, integrity, and consistent behavior are the foundations of "a good name," and that is becoming increasingly rare and valuable. Proverbs 22:1 declares, **"A good name is to be more desired than great wealth."** The meltdown of integrity, morality, discipline, and the devotion to truth has caused a rising hunger for the valuable qualities. The growing darkness and depression caused by the meltdown of trust will cause those who walk in the light to stand out more. As we see in Isaiah 60:1-3, which describes our times, the light wins. Ultimately, the nations will come to the light because it will stand out even more in the "deep darkness" we are now entering.

Again, one of the most important things we can do to be prepared for these times is resolve that we will not be taken over by the spirit of the age. Rather, we will have a different spirit. When trust in virtually everything is shaken, we must resolve that we will be trustworthy.

To be trustworthy means to be worthy of trust. As the world is becoming increasingly divided, the body of Christ will become increasingly unified. The Lord prayed for His people to be unified in John 17 so that the world would know that He was sent by The Father. Soon unity will be so rare that those who are in unity will stand out as a great light.

Unity must and will be built on trust. All relationships are built on trust. Trust is the bridge that connects us to each other. The weight of what can be carried across that bridge will depend on the strength of the trust. To grow in the unity that will be required to navigate these times will depend on each of us becoming more trustworthy, because our "yes" really does mean "yes" and our "no" really does mean "no."

Is not our faith in God the result of us having a history of His word being true? This is why the first attack of Satan was to get Adam and Eve to doubt God's word. If he can shake our trust in God's words, then he has shaken our trust in God. Therefore, if we are going to be trusted, we too must ensure that our words are true.

As we are resolved to be devoted to truth, we should be true first to ourselves, and then to our families, the church, and any group we might be a part of. Truth and trustworthiness will be most valuable commodities in these times of increasing chaos and confusion. Of this we can be sure.

We must also see the chaos and confusion of nations as the opportunities that they are for the Gospel of the kingdom. In the first mention of The Holy Spirit in Scripture, He is moving upon the chaos that this world once was. Look at the incredible creation that was brought forth out of the chaos! The Holy Spirit knows how to move upon chaos and bring order, beauty, and life.

As we see chaos and disorder increasing, we should expect The Holy Spirit to do something remarkable. Just as true warriors run to the sound of battle, not away from it, those who know The Holy Spirit will run to the chaos and confusion to see what He will do, and be available to Him to use them. He is "The Helper"—it is His nature to help, and so it will be with all who are filled with The Spirit. A main way that we can help now is to be devoted to truth and to The Spirit of Truth. If that is true with us then our "yes" will mean "yes," and our "no" will mean "no," every time.

To understand completely is to forgive completely. – *French proverb*

Chapter 24
The High Impact Life

Two primary ways we will find stability and order in these times of increasing chaos and disorder will be our moorings to The Scriptures as Christians and to our Constitution as citizens. Those who build their house upon The Rock and survive the coming storms will be those who know the Word and do it. Likewise, to bring stability back to our government, we must know our Constitution and adhere to it.

Those who find themselves elected to an office, or appointed to leadership today, tend to know little about what The Constitution says. Most are now more devoted to their own political ambitions or agenda, and so tend to be willing to bend or ignore The Constitution as much as is necessary for political expediency. In Scripture, this condition is called "lawlessness." It is one of the primary evils we are warned that we must face at the end of the age.

So, what can we do about it? As members of the body of Christ, we must determine that we will know the Word of God and obey it. And we must resolve that we will not follow or tolerate leaders who are not devoted to knowing the Word of God, and adhere to it. As citizens we must resolve that we will not continue to elect anyone who is not committed to The Constitution as the Supreme Law of the Land, and will actually defend it from enemies both foreign and domestic, not just say that they will.

Continuing the theme from a few chapters ago about how a child learns that it can manipulate and control others with their rage, this evil will grow with their age if a resolute leadership does not confront it and refuse to yield to it. As those grow who seek to manipulate and control others, the stakes get higher and the dangers increase.

History is full of examples of how this same kind of corruption of esteeming agendas and personal ambition above law grows in governments. The further it has been allowed to progress in our government, the more devastating the consequences will be for the nation. The ultimate result will be either the chaos of anarchy, or totalitarian control. As lawlessness gets more intolerable, most nations have chosen totalitarianism.

Psychologists once thought children that were not disciplined but rather reasoned with would grow up to be the most resistant to tyranny. However, they were shocked to find that the reverse was true. As the children matured, they so hungered for the order of discipline that they were drawn to those who were the most authoritarian. So, this is not how we prevent tyranny, but rather condition people to want it. This is why the breakdown of authority in schools has led to increasing lawlessness, and at the same time, a tendency for the lawless to seek authoritarian control.

Of course, those subject to abusive parents or other domineering authorities have been drawn to weaker, less threatening authority. Their wounds from abusive authority can make almost any exercise of the wisest authority seem threatening, and so they can be repelled by even the most loving, balanced authority. That does not mean that there is something wrong with the authority, but that these people have unhealed wounds from bad examples of authority that causes them to color all authority figures with this blurred vision.

We don't have time to dig into how some seriously flawed psychology is at the root of much of society's ills today, but even the greatest leadership can still be met with extreme reactions from people, and it is not the fault of the leaders. To heal a person who has learned to manipulate and control those around them with outrageous behavior is no small thing. Likewise, to heal a person who has been abused by authority is no small thing. To heal an entire population is obviously far more daunting, but is absolutely possible. However, it is only possible where there is liberty.

That is the challenge before us. It is beyond what any mere human leader can do. All that we are facing is not possible for us to fix, and is beyond human remedy, so we need God to heal our land. We must turn to Him, and we must keep in mind that nothing is impossible for Him.

Discipline helps us to develop internal guidelines and order. Not having discipline, and then being subject to whimsical and capricious leaders, is the recipe for deep internal discord and depression. This leads to such things as panic attacks and other extreme fear-based maladies. Children can come from very stable families but without proper, balanced discipline they can be capable of outrageous acts of lawlessness and cruelty, and seem to have little or no conscience about it. Likewise, populations can be well off in material things but be prone to deep darkness and depression without clear guidelines, both within and without. This leads to extreme social problems in a nation.

Now that we are facing this in our time, and it is increasing, we must keep in mind that the answer to lawlessness is not legalism, and the answer to legalism is not the removing of law or authority. There is a ditch on either side of the path of life. The ditch on one side is legalism. The ditch on the other is lawlessness. We must stay between the ditches. One way we do this if we are in a place of authority is for our "yes" to mean "yes" and "no" to mean "no" the first time we say it, and every time we say it.

The remarkable order in the universe is the result of it being upheld by the "word of His power." He is the stability of the universe because His word is dependable and never, ever fails. He always means what He says and fulfills His promises. We are called to be like Him, and so we too must have words that are true, and we must be true to our words. Those who are will have built their houses on The Rock. When the floods come they will stand and will be able to pull many others out.

Do not free a camel of the burden of his hump; you may be freeing him from being a camel. –*G.K. Chesterton*

Chapter 25
Faith is Power

When we understand how essential it is to believe God's Word and build our lives on adhering to it, we understand why the first lie of Satan was designed to cause doubt in God's Word. This caused the first fall and most of the falls since. This is why during orientation at most universities today, there will be a scathing assault on the validity of The Bible and on anyone who believes it. The devil knows that if he can shake a believer's faith in the Word of God, they will be easy prey and will fall.

Likewise, the strategy of those intent on destroying our Republic usually begin by sowing doubt about the legitimacy of The Constitution. Because we are a constitutional Republic, destroy The Constitution and you have destroyed the Republic because it no longer has a legitimate legal standing to be a government.

A direct frontal attack on The Constitution would be unlikely to work for those intent on destroying our Republic, just as it would not have worked for the devil to have told Adam and Eve outright that God lied to them. Satan is almost never that direct and neither are the enemies of our liberty. Like Satan, and maybe because he is the one working through them, the enemies of the Republic have worked hard to get us to doubt what The Constitution actually says or what the

Founders intended, just like he tries to get Christians to doubt The Scriptures.

Why should Satan change this strategy? It always seems to work. When it worked in the Garden, it threw the world into chaos. As it has worked in the church, it has been thrown into chaos. As he has done this in our government with The Constitution, the result is the chaos and dysfunction we now see every day in government. Without strong moorings to our foundations we will set adrift.

When just a few people woke up to what had been done to them through their doubt in God's Word, and they began to read The Bible with faith, it resulted in radical transformation of their world and times. The Reformation, or the reforming of the church that brought it out of "the dark ages," was born out of such revelation of just a few Scriptures coming to just a few people. This kind of power to change our world is not found anywhere else. The needed reformation in our government will come the same way, beginning with just a few seeing the light of what has happened to our country. It does not take many. As the great tipping points of change in history all reveal, a tiny percentage of the committed will prevail over the great majority that is asleep or indifferent.

Those who take serious things seriously, such as the foundation of our government and the continued fidelity to its integrity, can easily find out what the Founders meant by everything in The Constitution. Most of it is in *The Federalist Papers*. These were written by the authors of The Constitution in order to explain the main points in it to the states that had to ratify it. There are also many personal letters written still available by the Founders on what they intended in The Constitution.

So, anyone can know exactly what the Founders meant if they are willing to do a little research. But few are willing to read The Constitution, much less dig deeper into these additional resources. The result of our laziness is to have a most remarkable and precious gift of the best government ever devised stolen from us. Because so many have been too lazy to do a little study and stay informed, we are in worse danger of destruction than at any time in our history, and the cost of preserving our Republic is going up every day.

It is the same laziness of Christians who have not been willing to read The Bible that has allowed the church to become something closer to what the Book of Revelation called the "great harlot" and "Mystery Babylon"—rather than the chaste, spotless bride waiting faithfully for her King. However, there is an awakening beginning among Christians and among citizens. The future of both the church in America, and the American Republic itself, are dependent on this awakening continuing.

It has been said that "The future belongs to those who show up." The trajectory of our country was set by those who showed up and got engaged. We are told that **"The Spirit searches all things, even the depths of God" (see I Corinthians 2:10)**. Therefore, no one who is truly Spirit led will be shallow. Those filled with The Spirit will be like The Spirit, searching into the depths of what is important. The Spirit is also "The Spirit of Truth" that searches for truth, not just what we would agree with.

Yet, it is understood that not everyone has the time to research everything deeply. For this reason, I consider the time I have had to do this a sacred trust. I have spent years researching some things. I then put the conclusions of this research in books or resources like this that can be absorbed by others in hours. I'm honored to be able to do this for the household of God. However, it will still be those who use the time they have wisely—to check things out and do their due diligence to test what they read—who will find the treasures of wisdom and knowledge, and be the treasures in the times to come.

We are all in the same boat in a stormy sea, and we owe each other a terrible loyalty. –*G.K. Chesterton*

Chapter 26
Destroying Evil

In the first part of the dream I was given about the coming Second American Revolution/Civil War, great champions were released to go after specific evil strongholds. It was their work that enabled this coming Revolution/Civil War to be "successful." For this reason, we need to understand who these people are and how they will confront the evil strongholds of this time.

The word "champion" often brings thoughts of fit and strong athletes, but few of the ones in this dream were the athletic type. They were all ages, sexes, and types. I was almost seventy at the time, and I was not the oldest one there. I did not see any that physically looked like a warrior, but they all had a warrior's demeanor. None were novices—they were experienced and battle-hardened with an uncommon focus, resolve, and courage.

I don't think there is anything that can prevent any Christian from being one of these champions of the faith if they are serious, resolute disciples of Christ. What can prevent us from being one of these champions? Things like thinking you're too old. Remember that Abraham was too old when he was called, yet he became "the father of faith." Moses was eighty when he started his ministry. We are told that we have "a better covenant," so we should be able to do better than them.

This is not presumption, but rather having faith in God instead of having it in ourselves. There are only two things that can keep any serious disciple of Christ from being one of these champions:

1. They are too busy with the affairs of this life.

2. Like the ten evil spies that opposed Joshua and Caleb, they are more focused on how small they are rather than how big God is.

It was also apparent in this dream that the resolute focus of these champions did not happen overnight. Their life was one of preparation for their time. These were the soldiers who would be ready when The King called on them because they were not overly caught up in everyday affairs. These did not allow temporal things to eclipse the eternal purposes of God in their life. They will be ready when the Captain calls them, and they will fight like the great champions He has made them.

These champions in my dream were especially prepared for what they were about to do, but as they went forth, companies of people began to follow them. Even if we are not called to be a leader in a fight against these evil strongholds, we may be part of the company that follows them. Know your company, or tribe, and get in your place. Hear the sound of the trumpet call and respond.

When I was in the Navy, we each had a specific job to do and a specific duty station. If the ship was torpedoed, bombed, or suffered any kind of emergency, everyone became a part of the damage control teams. The obvious reason was that if the ship sank, all of our jobs would be gone, so dealing with the crisis became everyone's job. Our ship of state is now facing some of the biggest crises in our history, with attacks coming from within and without. Our ship of state is starting to sink, and almost everything we consider precious is being threatened. Therefore, getting engaged in this fight to save our ship must become a main priority of all until this danger has passed.

It is going to take the same kind of resolve and willingness to sacrifice to save our country that it took to found it. Our Founders risked their lives, their fortunes, and their sacred honor to give us the freedoms we have been so blessed with. Many gave their lives and their fortunes for our benefit, but they are numbered among those who will always be honored for their love and sacrifice. Now it is our turn to preserve what so many paid such a high price for so that this Republic is not lost on our watch.

As Christians we have dual citizenship. We are citizens of the kingdom of God and of the nation that He placed us in. These are not "either/or" responsibilities, but both together. Let there be no confusion about this—being true to both is being obedient to God.

For the coming times, the most important call going out will be to mobilize. We must each find our place in the great spiritual force that is being gathered. Then we must be taught, trained, equipped, and deployed. This force will become more defined, as well as the champions called to lead it. As this transformation takes place, those who will engage in the great battles of our times will not choose where they go to church based on superficial things like if they like the preacher, the worship, the children's ministry, etc. Rather, they will gather with those they are called to fight with in the great battles of our times, against the rising darkness of our times. Effective spiritual warfare will become increasingly crucial with each passing day.

Again, as we see in Ecclesiastes 3, there is a time for peace and a time for war. During peace the people will have a more peaceful demeanor, but during war there is a seriousness and a fierceness that comes over all. In this life we have always been in the most serious war of all—the battle for the souls of men. As the battle to save our Republic unfolds, a new awareness of the battle for the souls of the people will become clear. All of this is working to prepare the greatest spiritual force in history for the ultimate battle of the ages and the ultimate harvest of souls.

Am I not destroying my enemies when I make friends of them? *–Abraham Lincoln*

Chapter 27
The Revolution

There has not been another revolution in history like the American Revolution. It was led by the wealthiest in the land, not the most downtrodden. Those who signed the Declaration of Independence were among the top 1% of the wealthiest people in the colonies. They had more to risk than anyone, but they did not shrink back from risking all that they had.

The signers of the Declaration of Independence knew that they were risking all that they had, and even their lives. However, for two of them it was not just a risk—it was certain that they would lose all that they had the moment they signed the Declaration. British soldiers were camped right next to their estates and would no doubt seize them immediately. They signed anyway, and they immediately lost everything they had worked their entire lives to build. They lost everything except their honor and an eternal reward. That honor will be worth more than any fortune in eternity. Fortunes cannot be carried beyond this life, but noble deeds will be remembered forever.

The great fortunes of many today were given to them for this same purpose—to save their country. Does anyone have something better to do with it? Almost all the bigger homes, cars, planes, or yachts will soon be lost anyway if those seeking the destruction of our Republic are successful. We do not want to be remembered for failing to use what we have when it is needed.

Haym Salomon was a Jewish immigrant from Poland to the American colonies, and he became one of the greatest heroes of the Revolutionary War, even though he did not fight in any battle. He had become a businessman and financier, but also one of the great American patriots. His crucial part was to pay for the Continental Army's supplies throughout the Revolutionary War, but his biggest contribution came in 1781.

When General Washington saw the opportunity to trap the British Army at Yorktown, he had no supplies and the coffers for his army were empty. He told his staff to "Contact Haym Salomon." Salomon quickly provided the money to buy the needed supplies for the Continental Army's march to Virginia, where the British army was defeated, and the war was won.

It is hard to verify today where Salomon got the money, but there is evidence he gave his own fortune—all of it. He was also never repaid by the Continental Congress. Even so, the Star of David was placed on the dollar bill in his honor. Even more so, such deeds are not forgotten in heaven.

The American Republic Haym Salomon helped found with his fortune became the primary supporter of the founding of the modern State of Israel. For this reason, from heaven's perspective, Haym Salomon is not just considered a Founding Father of the American Republic, but also of Israel. We reap what we sow for good or bad, and it seems the great champion of the first American Revolution, Haym Salomon, is being repaid with interest as America has been the primary financial supporter of Israel.

What can we invest to help preserve this Republic that many sacrificed so much to establish, and countless more gave even their lives to preserve in their time? It must not be lost on our watch. It is now our time to stand up. It is again a time for heroes of the faith to arise and demonstrate their faith. Who knows, maybe even the small part we might play in this is the part that starts to turn the tide.

The Republic will be restored, but will we be a part? Or will we be Rip van Winkle and sleep through a great revolution? "It is always the right time to do the right thing." Now is the time to stand up and be counted with the great souls of every generation that have stood up.

If we are not a great champion then we must find one to get behind and support. As King David, about whom it was said that he was a man after God's heart, or that he had a heart like God's, he established that the supporters of the army that stayed behind with the baggage should get the same reward as those who went to the battle. The warriors could not go to the battle without those who supported them behind the front. Even if we are not one of the champions, we can receive the same reward by supporting them.

The great champions of the faith throughout the ages have all had one common denominator: they did not look at how small and inadequate they were, but at how big their God was. We would only consider ourselves too old or too anything if we are looking at ourselves as the source instead of having faith in God.

As we look at the great darkness of our times, which according to Scripture will be the darkest it has been since Noah, we have the greatest opportunity of all time to see how powerful our God is. Let us seize this incredible time in which we have been chosen to live. Great victories require great battles, and the last battle will be the greatest of all.

Even if we failed often, and shrank back from standing up as we should have until now, to have stood against the great darkness of these times is the greatest opportunity of all to be named among the great heroes of the faith. The past is gone.

It no longer exists. Now is the time, now is the day of our salvation. Now is the time to resolve that we will not retreat any further before the darkness, but rather we will take our stand and not surrender another inch to the enemies of the cross, regardless of the cost.

The victory will come from those who arise with faith in God. Age, strength, education, and other natural abilities are not major factors in this battle. Faith in God, not ourselves, is the greatest factor now. Will we believe in the One with whom nothing is impossible? If we do, we can probably count on our weaknesses being what qualifies us. He loves to use the weak to confound the strong, the simple to confound the wise. Yet, to be used by Him we must believe in Him. If we see Him, who He is and where He sits above all rule and authority and dominion, and that He has sent us, we cannot fail if we do not quit.

Artists are the real architects of change, and not the political legislators who implement change after the fact. –*William S. Burroughs*

Either write something worth reading or do something worth writing. –*Benjamin Franklin*

Chapter 28
Righteous Anger

As covered, in the dream I had about the Second American Revolution/Civil War, I saw that different people were called to go after different strongholds. They received their call by teeing off on a golf course. The thing that "tees you off" the most is a way you will know what you have been called to fight. If there is a deep anger, a provoking of your spirit about a specific evil, then consider this a call of God. It is time to get to your post and get in the fight.

Living waters come from "the innermost being." Those in Christ have both positive and negative callings, just as Jesus did. We're told that He went about doing good, and we're also told that He came to "destroy the works of the devil." Of course, we would like to just do the fun part, the doing of good, but we are all called to destroy the works of the enemy. If we shrink back from either of these we will not fulfill our ultimate purpose.

In Isaiah 60:18, The Lord said of Jerusalem that He would call her gates praise and her walls salvation. When the exiles returned to rebuild the destroyed city, they had to rebuild the walls with a trowel in one hand and a sword in the other. There are times when we have to build and fight at the same time. If they had not been willing to fight, they would have never finished with the building, and neither will we.

As we read in Ecclesiastes 3, there is a time for everything—a time for peace and a time for war. It is time for war. How could it ever not be when we are told that **"the whole world lies in the power of the evil one" (see I John 5:19)**. Yet, God's army, one of the major characteristics of the body of Christ that we are called to be, is hardly reflected anywhere in the body of Christ. This is about to change. There will be a military organization and demeanor coming to the advancing church that will be a striking difference from what it has been before.

My default spiritual weapon is to write or speak about what I have been given. When I had the dream about the coming Second American Revolution/Civil War, I immediately inquired of The Lord about what I could write or teach that would help us to get ready. He said that I had already done this. I immediately knew why I was so compelled to write the *Army of the Dawn* books, and I was told to put everything else I was working on aside until they were finished. These books are the result of the many years I spent studying military history, and they contain the practical aspects of what it will take for the church to become the army we are called to be.

This may seem like a shameless plug for these books, and it may be, but I can't be concerned about that now. We are in desperate need of becoming all that we have been called to be as His people, and that especially means the army we are called to be. Those books are even more prophetic than I realized. You can find them in many bookstores, or order them directly from our bookstore website at: store.morningstarministries.org.

I have now written nearly seventy-five books and booklets. As I reviewed these, I was surprised that almost all of them were in some way about us becoming the spiritual army we are called to be and about the conflict we are now entering. That has obviously been a core of the message I have been given. In my search for those I can help along their way, I have always looked for those with the spirit of a warrior, and it seems that those who are the most attracted to our ministry are of this nature. I know my part and this is it.

Few realize that in a modern army about 80% of the personnel are the support of the 20% that actually are on the front lines engaging the enemy. On the aircraft carrier I was on we had about 5,500 on the ship, but only 200-300 were flight crews who were actually to engage the enemy. All the rest did what was necessary to get the ship in the right place so these flight crews could get in the fight, but everyone on that ship knew that everyone was crucial for us to be the force we had to be. The same is true in the body of Christ.

The peace of God is one of our main weapons for us to be the spiritual army we are called to be. Love, truth, justice, and all of the other characteristics the citizens of the kingdom of God are called to have are our "divinely powerful weapons." To use all of these effectively, we must add to them the characteristics of the military demeanor we're called to have, such as training (not just teaching), organization that enables coordinated action, strategic thinking, clear objectives, etc.

Because these are all covered in the *Army of the Dawn* books, I will not go any deeper here, but we must move resolutely in this direction as the body of Christ to be prepared for these times in order to prevail in them and not be overcome.

As the Great Commission is to disciple all nations, not just individuals, we must understand and engage in doing this. To understand how we are to do this with the American Republic, we must start with understanding the foundations that were laid and build upon them properly.

I spent years studying our nation's history with one Scripture as my inspiration and motive, Psalm 90:16-17:

Let Your work appear to Your servants and Your majesty to their children.

Let the favor of the Lord our God be upon us; and confirm for us the work of our hands; yes, confirm the work of our hands.

I began my study in order to see the work of The Lord in the founding, building, and vision of our nation. It was not hard to find. When I saw it, I then sought The Lord's favor to confirm the work that we are called to do to see our national destiny fulfilled.

As we are told in Proverbs 4:18, "The path of the righteous (or the right path) is like the light of dawn, that shines brighter and brighter until the full day." The path I walked seeking to find and understand our Divine purpose as a nation was like this—it just kept getting brighter. It was like discovering a mother lode of truth and wisdom.

You may not have the time I had to do this research, but if you do what you can and ask The Lord to be your Guide, your Teacher, He will. The payoff is to be able to move with clarity and boldness to fulfill our own purpose in this, and together our national purpose and our purpose as the body of Christ to prepare the way for The Lord.

You never change things by fighting the existing reality. To change something, build a new model that makes the existing model obsolete. –*R. Buckminster Fuller*

Chapter 29
A Constitutional Crisis

As we have covered, virtually every crisis that the American Republic is now facing is the result of disregarding The Constitution, which is "the supreme law of the land." The parallel in the church is striking. Virtually every crisis in the U.S. church is the result of a disregard of our founding document— The Bible. In both cases, the ultimate answer to fixing these problems is to return to the founding documents—studying them, knowing them, and adhering to them.

A complicating factor is the general deception that is like a veil cast over the whole world. It is so pervasive that few can discern truth. Some of those screaming the loudest about the violations to The Constitution are the worst violators. Likewise, many who decry the departure from the sound doctrine of The Scriptures can be some of the biggest violators.

Politicians could not get away with this if citizens were knowledgeable and informed about The Constitution. Neither could the Christian leaders get away with such twisting of Scripture if believers were knowledgeable of them. This has led to what The Lord warned about through Isaiah 5:13, **"Therefore My people go into bondage for their lack of knowledge."**

What can be done to change the ignorance and deception that is so pervasive now? A lot. Because the darkness is now so deep, any little light can shine like a great beacon. Any Christian who takes their stand on a single truth could be a major part in turning the tide against the prevailing deception.

As Malcolm Gladwell pointed out in his classic work *The Tipping Point*, the percentage of people needed to bring about profound change is the square root of one percent of the population. This means that just one hundred people can bring radical change to a million.

This equation has been proven repeatedly in history. Some of the most profound changes have come by a much smaller percentage. Look at what The Lord did with just twelve! This means that if just those of you who read this become knowledgeable, informed, and discerning, we would have many times as many people as would be needed to bring about a profound change in the U.S.

What are we waiting for?

One of the delusions those in democracies come under is thinking they need a majority of the people to accomplish anything significant. That is a major deception stopping many from doing their part, which they see as small or insignificant. First, we need to understand that what needs to be done is not going to happen by a vote. It is going to happen the way that our Republic was founded—by the spreading of powerful ideas that capture the hearts of the people who will take action. In the case of our first revolution, the percentage of people for independence never grew to more than 30% of the population, and only a small fraction of this group ever engaged in an actual battle.

As The Lord showed Gideon, sometimes we try to accomplish things with too many people. The laws that govern great and transcendent change are similar to poker—four of a kind beats a full house. Unity is far more powerful than numbers.

Just about every new political movement in America claims a "grassroots" strategy, which means to influence the multitudes. Most of these movements die from the discouragement of not reaching the great numbers they expected. This is a wrong strategy. As demented as Karl Marx was he got one thing right—it only takes a small fraction of the passionate to take over the multitudes that are indifferent.

Neither does it take much time to get educated on our founding documents. If we took as much time to feed our inner man with daily manna from The Bible as we spend cleaning and trying to make our outer man look good, we would likely have been Bible scholars and powerful preachers a long time ago. If we read just four chapters of The Bible a day, we would read it entirely in less than a year. Then we would immediately know if what preachers and teachers are proclaiming is true or not.

It is even easier with our national founding documents because we can read them in just a couple of hours. It takes more study to grasp the insights, but there are scholars who have spent years studying the applications and deviations of The Constitution and have put them in books we can read in just a few hours. If we spent just fifteen minutes a day reading these, within a year we would have a very strong foundation for understanding what is being done to us by our present government leaders.

The American Republic has not failed us, but we have failed the Republic. We can have the best form of government but still have bad government if we do not have good people in it. At the root of the crisis that now threatens the continued existence of our Republic is the way that we choose those who run for office. It is a process that the best potential leaders in the country will not get involved in because it is so contrary to what would bring out the best leadership. Our present process rewards compliance and loyalty to the party above competence and loyalty to the country.

This is parallel to the way leaders are now chosen in the church. Loyalty to a denomination or a movement can eclipse our loyalty to Christ. In both the spiritual and the natural we must return to and strengthen ourselves in the only foundations that will stand.

What would happen if we took just a little of the time now consumed by watching mindless and meaningless sitcoms or other programs, and spent it being responsible Christians and responsible citizens? The critical changes that must come if we are to survive as a Republic, and become the force the body of Christ is called to be, would come swiftly.

What do we have to do that is more important than this? Have we become like Esau who sold his birthright for the quick and temporary gratification of his flesh? Remember that Esau is the only individual in Scripture that God said he despised. As the Apostle Paul wrote in II Timothy 2:3-4:

> **Suffer hardship with me, as a good soldier of Christ Jesus.**
>
> **No soldier in active service entangles himself in the affairs of everyday life, so that he may please the one who enlisted him as a soldier.**

Are we good soldiers of Christ Jesus, or are we like Esau? Do we realize that the word "entertainment" came from merging the words *"to detain from entering."* Presently, there may be nothing on earth that is robbing more people of their eternal rewards in Christ like entertainment.

Recreation is different from entertainment. Recreation comes from re-creation, and it does help to renew physically and spiritually. This is not to imply that any entertainment is sin, or bad, but when it becomes a big part of what we give our free time to, it is robbing us and must be replaced by things that edify us.

It is noteworthy that The Lord said that a centurion, a professional soldier, had more faith than anyone in Israel. It is also noteworthy that another centurion was chosen to be the first among the Gentiles to receive the Gospel and The Holy Spirit. There is something of a military mentality that can help us comprehend spiritual realities better than anything else.

At any given time, less than 1% of the U.S. population is in the military. So, only a small percentage of citizens get to experience the discipline of military life. How are the rest able to get this experience? If the church were to become what it is called to be, every Christian would get this. It is called "discipleship," the only New Testament method for preparing leaders and maturing all believers.

The Great Commission is to make disciples, not just converts. The Lord was very specific about what His disciples would be like, and if we examined His teachings on this we may conclude that we do not know any true disciples. This must be recovered if we are going to fulfill our purpose in these times.

Again, because this is covered in the two volume *Army of the Dawn* series, I will not belabor this more here. On November 3, 2020 I had a face-to-face encounter with The Lord. He spoke to me about the coming of His kingdom and the Gospel of His kingdom that yet had to be preached. During a pause when it seemed He wanted me to ask a question, I asked what the main thing was that we could do to help prepare for His coming kingdom. Without hesitation He said, "Make disciples."

There have been numerous attempts by movements to make disciples that have gone awry, just as almost every other biblical truth has been distorted and taken to extremes by some. In this encounter, this was going through my mind as The Lord continued to pause as if to have me ask Him about this. I then asked Him the main thing we could do to make disciples that would help us stay on track with it. His response was, "Start."

First, it is a delusion of pride for us to think that we are going to do anything perfectly, but as we addressed earlier about the law of inertia, it is impossible to steer anything that is not moving. If we will start, do what we think is right to do, and keep the humility that keeps us open to correction, even our mistakes will be used for good. If we keep in mind that we are only a small part of His army, and only know what we do in part so as to stay open to what others are learning, we will soon see Christians becoming what they are called to be and doing what they are called to do.

The whole history of the progress of human liberty shows that all concessions yet made to her august claims have been born of earnest struggle...If there is no struggle, there is no progress... Power concedes nothing without a demand...Find out just what any people will quietly submit to and you have found out the exact measure of injustice and wrong which will be imposed upon them...The limits of tyrants are prescribed by the endurance of those whom they oppress. –*Frederick Douglass*

Chapter 30
The Holy Nation

The biblical "holy nation" is a nation within all nations—it is the true church, the body of Christ. This holy nation has its own destiny and purpose, one aspect of which is to help all nations become what they were created to be, and thereby holy to The Lord.

The American Republic has arisen to, in some ways, become the greatest nation in history. This has not happened without mistakes and tragedies that we must also acknowledge. We still have many flaws. Even so, we have been the dominant economic and military force in the world for over half a century, and yet have rarely used it to dominate others and impose our will on them.

I say "rarely" here because there have been times and places when we have used it to force our will on others. However, there has never been a nation that rebuilds its enemies after defeating them in war as has the U.S. As one leader of a developing nation said, "The quickest way for a nation to prosper is to go to war with the United States, surrender quickly, and then watch the aid pour in."

The American Republic may have been the most generous nation in history. We are known for being the quickest and most generous to respond to a natural disaster anywhere in the world, even if they take place in countries considered our enemies.

Though we have had many inconsistencies and hypocrisy in the way we allowed slavery, treated the American Indians, and then continued to oppress minorities, we have confronted much of this evil and continue to make progress. There is much in our history that is honorable, and we would be unjust not to "give honor to whom honor is due."

With all of the good that has been done, and the mistakes we have learned so much from, there are now two crises in America that will destroy our Republic if not addressed quickly. The Founders warned about both of these threats, saying that if either got a grip on the country then the Republic would be doomed. They now have more than a grip—they have a stranglehold on us.

The first and most serious of these threats was what Thomas Jefferson called "judicial tyranny." Even in the first years of the new nation, he saw a creeping tendency for the judicial branch to usurp the authority of the other two branches, as well as that of the states and the people. The judicial has now done this in clear violation of The Constitution.

In regard to this judicial tyranny, we have now surpassed what the Founders feared could happen—in some ways it has surpassed judicial tyranny to become judicial anarchy. The Constitution is now hanging by a thread.

A shocking example of this judicial tyranny was the way federal judges blocked Executive Orders by President Trump. This is about as clear a violation of the "separation of powers" in The Constitution as we may have ever had. The Executive Orders nullified by these judges were within the authority given to the President by both The Constitution and the Congress through legislation. These judges made a direct assault on the authority of both the President and the Congress by blocking these Executive Orders. These rogue judges did not cite any violation of The Constitution or any laws for their actions—they just disagreed with the President's policy.

There are hundreds of federal judges. What if they all started blocking any law or policy they disagreed with? Because the Judicial branch has become so politicized, if conservative judges began to block any law or Executive Order they did not agree with, and every liberal judge started doing the same, no law could be passed or enforced, and no executive actions could be taken. If they have the power to block any law of Congress or Executive Order by the President, they have basically nullified the authority of both the other branches of government and made themselves the supreme law of the land in place of The Constitution.

It is a fallacy that The Constitution established three *co-equal* branches of government. This was never intended, and it was not done. The Constitution mandates three branches that were intended to have checks and balances on each other, but they were never intended to be co-equal in authority. The Constitution gave the Legislative branch the most authority because it was expected to be the most responsive to the states and the people. This is why it is the only branch given the authority to impeach and to control government spending.

The second most powerful branch of government was the Executive branch, which was given the authority over national defense and foreign policy. Obviously, not all three branches of government could have their own foreign policy, but this is what the judicial sought to assume by attacking President Trump's immigration orders.

Immigration was placed under foreign policy, and thereby is the Executive branch's sole domain. For individual federal judges, who were not elected but rather appointed, to assume authority over the President and the Congress with their actions is one of the most egregious violations of The Constitution in our history.

Whether we agreed with President Trump's policies or not, the federal judges that put stays on his Executive Orders should have been immediately impeached for such a blatant violation of The Constitution and separation of powers. This did not happen because of inept leadership in Congress, which alone has the power to impeach.

Without question there must be a strong and independent judiciary for there to be justice in the land, but the judicial has now gotten so far out of its lane—usurping the authority of the other two branches of the federal government, as well as the authority that was to remain with the states and the people— that it is now the biggest threat to the Republic, just as the Founders predicted.

So, what can we do? Start to take back the legitimate authority that we the people have as the sovereign in our Republic, and even more importantly, the authority that the King of kings gave us to do what we are here to do. "Suppose that Satan succeeds because we, as Christians, fail to fulfill our responsibilities. What then? Jesus Himself gave us the answer. We become salt that has lost its savor. He warned us of the fate that awaits such savorless salt: **"It is thenceforth good for nothing, but to be cast out, and to be trodden under foot of men" (Matthew 5:13).**

If we in the church fail to hold back the forces of wickedness, our judgment is to be handed over to those very forces. –*Derek Prince*

Beloved, we are convinced of better things concerning you, and things that accompany salvation, though we are speaking in this way.

For God is not unjust so as to forget your work and the love which you have shown toward His name, in having ministered and in still ministering to the saints.

And we desire that each one of you show the same diligence so as to realize the full assurance of hope until the end,

so that you will not be sluggish, but imitators of those who through faith and patience inherit the promises (Hebrews 6:9-12).

PARTNERS

Our MorningStar Partners have grown into an extraordinary global fellowship of men and women who are committed to seeing The Great Commission fulfilled in our times. Join us in equipping the body of Christ through conferences, schools, media, and publications.

We are committed to multiplying the impact of the resources entrusted to us. Your regular contribution of any amount—whether it's once a month or once a year—will make a difference!

In His Service,

PARTNER WITH US TODAY

MSTARPARTNERS.ORG
1-844-JOIN-MSP